KNIFE CHILDREN

KNIFE CHILDREN

A novella in the world of *The Sharing Knife*

Lois McMaster Bujold

Subterranean Press 2020

Lois McMaster
BUJOLD

First Hardcover Edition

ISBN
978-1-59606-954-1

Subterranean Press
PO Box 190106
Burton, MI 48519

subterraneanpress.com

Manufactured in the United States of America

KNIFE CHILDREN

BARR scraped his knife over his face by feel, delicately razoring off the last of his tawny beard. He had been pretty proud of that beard, not to mention grateful for its protection when patrolling in the harsh Luthlian winters, but exuberant spring had hit the hinterland of Oleana at just about the time he'd ridden over the border six days back. The muggy heat smelled like new life, like the shy green of the woods around him. It smelled like home. He drew a deep, deep breath of it, and exhaled the last of snowy exile.

Tossing the double handful of springy beard hairs atop the pile of bay clumps he'd curried out of his mare, he left them all for the birds. Breaking camp consisted merely of kicking the dirt over the embers of his fire, rolling his blanket tight, and saddling up. Briar snorted sleepily as he swung into his well-worn saddle and turned her onto the one-horse-wide patrol trail he'd been following. If he remembered aright, it should drop down to cross the farmer road in just a few more miles.

He might have made Pearl Riffle Camp already but for this familiar little detour, a few days out of his way. His tent-kin could only have a vague idea of his expected arrival; he could slip in this personal patrol unseen and so uncommented-upon. *Especially uncommented-upon.* He dismissed a lingering guilty twinge as something aged out of use. A dozen and more years his secret had kept itself. Now there was only the routine of tending to this private watch, to be renewed with his return from his two years of exchange patrolling in the far north.

The cart width of the farmer road came up right on time, and he swung his mount southward onto it. He unfurled his groundsense to its fullest extent, taking in the fresh world around him and all its spring-swelling life...the sun-speckled woodlands, the rising sap of the new plants almost as busy as the scurry of the awakening animals, the dark hum of the soil, and even, when he let his mind ease open and listened with utmost quietude, that subtlest song of the underlying stone itself. He hadn't been able to sense so deep down before he'd gone on his exchange.

He was pleased to confirm that his range, too, had grown, well over half a mile in every direction. Not far short of his friend and sometimes-mentor Dag Bluefield with his awesome full mile—they'd have to compare, when Barr next visited upriver to Clearcreek. But Pearl Riffle first. And before Pearl Riffle, this.

The first peopled farmsteads came into his groundsense, and soon into his sight. He twitched Briar aside to make way for a cart of well-rotted winter manure that its farmer driver aimed to spread on the next field. Barr cast him a polite salute. The man, identifying the rider as a Lakewalker patroller, scowled warily back, but tipped his straw hat in return politeness. He twisted to look over his shoulder as Barr rode on, and Barr hardly needed groundsense to feel the suspicion. That was one thing about home that hadn't changed much in two years, more's the pity. Lakewalker practices were a lot less secret than they had used to be, but sometimes Barr thought that just gave rumor more to distort. A trifle wounded, if only in his feelings, Barr pulled his perception back into himself, reminded again why Lakewalkers kept their extra senses closed around their farmer neighbors. Mostly.

A spur of hill bent the road in a curve, and on its other side Barr found the big woodlot that had served him so well as a hide over the years. He rode in until the whipping branches grew too punishing, then dismounted and led his mare down to the rivulet that divided the woods. He unbridled and watered her, leaving her with a compulsion not to stray. Groundsense half-open to detect any occupants well before they could notice him, he slipped through the woods toward the rise that gave him the best view of what he'd long thought of as *Lily's farm*, though the man who owned it called it after himself; so, the Mason place, in local talk. Fiddler Mason was Lily's mother's husband.

Though not, Barr reflected ruefully, Lily's father. Not being a Lakewalker, the man fortunately had no way to tell this.

Being a Lakewalker, Barr unfortunately did.

He'd been eighteen, just woken to what he'd naively imagined to be his full powers as a new patroller. The same beguiling persuasion that worked on animals worked on farmers, he'd heard, and, encountering that pretty young farmer girl when his patrol had camped on her family's land, he'd been more than tempted to try it out. Bluebell hadn't been unwilling. He'd not mistaken those artful glances of admiration she'd cast his youthful good looks. From admiration to arousal turned out to be but a step, and a step more from there to the loft of her father's barn. Where he'd tried his best to give her as good a time as what he now recognized as his clumsy inexperience could provide.

Her older sister had disapproved, though not enough to tattle on her to their parents. Barr's patrol partner Remo had disapproved even more, vehemently rejecting Barr's suggestion that Remo take on the sister as well, in case it was jealousy. (On either side, Barr had barely had the wits not to say.) Really, the two'd had so much in common... But Remo hadn't tattled to their patrol leader, either.

And Barr had ridden away thinking little more on it, and then even less as events overtook him and Remo both. They'd returned from their epic trip to the sea and back much-changed patrollers, older in more than years.

So when, at Barr's next routine patrol through these parts, he'd chanced upon the now-married Bluebell and her two-year-old, blond daughter, the shock of recognition had staggered him. *My child,* the tow-headed toddler's ground showed, unmistakably. After being roundly told off by Bluebell and commanded to keep away from her and hers forever, Barr had ridden away rocked by churning thoughts.

He'd taken his confusion to Dag and Fawn Bluefield, the only Lakewalker-farmer couple he knew, pleading for advice. Where he'd got his head washed by Fawn all over again, as she'd backed up Bluebell's demand in the sharpest terms. She'd also delivered him a homily on the realities of farmer-women's lives, illustrated with some eye-opening tales from her own younger days that'd left him cringing.

Dag was plain-spoken, but had a deadly aim. His time as a patrol captain had taught him everything about young patrollers he might've missed in being one, and their shared ordeals on the big river trip had shown him precisely where to put the knife into Barr for the most effect. *Why we do not use Lakewalker persuasion on farmers for sexual favors, ever,* yeah, that scar could still bleed when Barr poked at it.

Not that he hadn't had that lecture from his own patrol leaders, but Dag'd had a way of making it *stick.* Or maybe it was their joint witness of that evil Lakewalker renegade Crane, ruling his gang of river bandits, surely at the bottom of the slippery slope Barr had slithered along the top of. He remembered a ravine full of bodies, and shuddered.

Barr had never strayed off the marked trail again, that was certain. Which didn't mean the consequences of the first-and-last time didn't keep spinning out.

Because, Dag had allowed, Lily needed keeping an eye on not just for her general welfare, but in case she threw to her Lakewalker bloodline and experienced some frightening rise of groundsense when she grew from girl to woman.

At one time, Barr had almost hoped that would happen, if only to prove…something, maybe about himself to himself, some Lakewalkerish potency or other blighted nonsense. A longer stretch rubbing about the world had robbed him of such self-centered views. If Lily were lucky, she would inherit no more than a usefully keen intuition, and go on blending with her family and neighbors all unsuspected. And maybe find happiness, in some short-lived farmerish way.

As the years slid by without sign or rumor of anything strange about the pretty oldest Mason girl, Barr had slowly relaxed. She'd not yet started her monthlies, barely budding, when Barr had been assigned to exchange in Luthlia, a valuable training experience for a powerful young Lakewalker destined, maybe, for patrol leader soon. Lily had been just fine then; checking on her closely, or as closely as he could without being spotted, was the last task he'd done on his way out of Oleana.

And the first on his return.

Settling behind some deadfall at the edge of the woodlot, he let his perception stretch to a hundred or so paces, looking for the daily routines of the farm. And for Lily. She might be out feeding the animals, planting the kitchen garden, helping in the orchard. Or inside, plucking a chicken or cooking in the kitchen, or spinning. Or, most likely, pressed to look after her string of little brothers and sisters that had appeared with calendrical regularity, as if Bluebell were trying to make up her initial lie to her oblivious spouse by sheer weight of numbers.

Not that it mattered materially, given the patrilinear farmer passion for their lands. Lily's half-brother Reeve, as Fid's eldest boy, would inherit the Mason farm in due course. Not Lily. Lily would be expected to go be the wife on someone else's farm. *She should have been my tent-heiress.*

Barr's reaching groundsense found...no one.

Huh?

He stood from his concealing crouch, blinking and staring.

The house and barn were burned to the ground, only a few blackened timbers and a chimney still sticking up. A more distant shed and, as if in mockery, the privy still stood. Not a person, not a farm animal, not even a stray dog skulked about.

Barr lurched forward to the ruins, jaw hanging open. The char was cold, rain-sodden, a few sly weeds starting to creep in around the edges of the burn. The smoke-stink was old. Not a recent disaster, then; a month or two gone? *No blight sign,* he stifled his first surge of panic. *Not a malice attack.* Ground-ripping wasn't the only force that could level a place, even if it was the most absolute. *People can die just as hard from other things, you know.*

But neither eye nor groundsense found any human bodies in the shambles, although at the barn he was able to make out the remains of a couple of sheep, pulled apart and mostly disposed of by some later wild scavengers, foxes or vultures or crows. Belly-cold, he walked along the path to the home graveyard at the edge of the woods, stride lengthening as he made out the mound of a new-turned grave. It bore no marker, or none yet. Was it too short to harbor an adult...?

Blight it, *he* was the one who was supposed to be riding into mortal danger. Not *her*. Lily was supposed to be left *safe* here...

He stood shaken and bewildered for a moment more. *No.* He rubbed his mouth. It couldn't be as much a mystery around these parts as it was to him. People in the village would have to know what had happened, where the Mason family had gone. He'd always been chary about asking too many questions around Lily's village, because people tended to remember the overly curious Lakewalker stranger. But he'd have to ask now. He hurried back to his horse.

She was supposed to be safe...

WITH AS MANY as a couple of dozen horses in an average patrol, the one sort of farmer regularly visited by Lakewalkers on their twice-yearly rounds was the village blacksmith. Barr had encountered the Hackberry Corner man several times by now, both on official patrols and during his more private reconnoiters. The smith was either unusually open-minded about what farmers named, not without some cause, *Lakewalker necromancy,* or the patrols'

regular custom bought his tolerance. Barr had always found the smith a reliable if rambling source of local gossip.

The smithy's doors were pushed wide to the spring air, the whanging of metal on metal betraying why. Barr dismounted and ventured in, then paused. Hot iron waited on no man.

The coals of the forge glowed dully under a coat of gray, muted by the block of sunlight streaming in. The smith was swinging his hammer on a long piece held in place, somewhat to Barr's surprise, by a sturdy young woman in a leather apron whom he recognized as the smith's daughter. She turned it steadily between blows as it slowly deformed in the desired direction. The man let his hammer droop, stood up drawing breath, and waved at the forge. The girl tucked the cooling end neatly back into the coals, then went around to work the bellows.

The smith, whose name, memorably enough, was Smith, turned to Barr. "Well, how de', Lakewalker. Haven't seen you around for a while."

Barr ducked his head in return greeting. "I was gone to Luthlia. Just on my way back home."

Smith's bushy brows went up. "That's a long ways."

"Having just rode every mile of it, I have to agree."

"Horseshoes worn?"

"Not to change out yet. But as I was riding through, I saw the Mason place had burned down." The buildings, or their remains, were not at all visible from the road, nor was this village exactly on the route to Pearl Riffle, but Barr glided lightly over those wrinkles. "What the blight happened there, and when?"

"Ah." Smith brightened right up. Hackberry Corner was a place short of entertainment; fires and like disasters could be a fruitful source of gossip for years, after. Or maybe the blacksmith was just especially fond of blazes. "That was a right mess, and a tragedy, too, as it turned out."

Barr stiffened, resisting the urge to grab the fellow by his sweaty collar and tell him to get on with it. He managed a neutral but still encouraging, "Oh?"

"Kid playing with candles in the barn in the evening, was how it started, I heard. On accident, but still. *Which* kid was the source of the row, later, since the girl said it was the boy, and the boy said it was the girl, but in any case, it jumped to the house, and then it was too late for anything. Though Fid and Bell tried. They did get all the youngsters out, and most of the animals, so there's that. But by the time the neighbors saw the glow against the sky and smoke and ran over, there was nothing left to do but watch it finish burn."

"*Which* girl and boy?" Barr got out.

"Yeah, Fid and Bell's got a passel of them, don't they? The oldest girl, Lily, and the second boy, Edjer. Who'd always been a handful, got to say. I'm inclined to Lily's story, myself. But the boy took a lung fever from all the smoke, and was carried off inside a week, poor tyke. The family was real shook by that, when they thought they'd all got out clear except for Fid's burns. Bell didn't much care for Lily sticking to her story against the dead boy. Which I can kind of understand, though it don't seem fair. I mean, if it really was Ed started it. Not so much if it was the other way around."

Not Lily, not Lily, *not Lily* in that short grave. Barr, dizzied, concealed his huff of profound relief.

He opened his mouth, but the smith's daughter called, "Pa, it's ready," and Smith motioned Barr to wait. Barr stood back. This time, the girl took the hammer and her father turned the piece. The hammer whanged all the same, the sparks spurting in orange sprays.

"More to the end," Smith called, and, "Good! Stop there for now." He quenched the rod in a nearby barrel of water. A female voice called something unintelligible from the adjacent house, and Smith added, "Go see what your ma wants." The girl nodded and scampered off.

"You apprenticing her?" Barr couldn't help asking.

"Yep." Smith nodded in a satisfied way. "She'd been hanging around underfoot all her life, but I'd thought her older brother was going to take over from me. Except he was wild to go on the river, which his ma thought was too dangerous. I told him it wasn't going to be any less work, neither. We butted heads for a long time, till I finally gave up and let him go. I think he could be surprised, if he ever comes dragging back here, to find the forge didn't wait for him. Meggie's half my partner already. I give her all the fiddly bits, which she's got a better eye for than me, I must say it what shouldn't, her ma says."

Barr was then dragged aside to dutifully inspect and admire some sample fiddly bits, a right elegant set of ivy-leaf iron hinges and a three-fourths finished spray of copper flowers intended to crown a door lintel. But at last he was able to bring the gossip back around to his own most burning paternal interest.

"So where are all the Masons now? There was no one around their place. Are they coming back?"

"Oh, they was all took in by Bell's sister Iris, down at her place. It makes for a mob, with all those cousins, but family deals as family must. Soon as Fid recovers a bit more, village plans a house-raising for them. And maybe a barn-raising come fall. It won't be a patch on the ones that burned down, but it'll be a start. They need something before Bell pops her next one."

"She's pregnant again?"

"Oh, aye. Fid says she catches like a fishing net, without hardly trying."

All right, maybe it wasn't just me…

Though Lakewalkers tended to the opposite problem about fertility. Had those assumptions ambushed Barr, back then, made him careless? *Nh.* At that age, his notions of long-term consequences had come to something like *tomorrow's sundown,* so maybe not. "I wonder if she hopes it'll be a boy to make up?"

"I don't think it works quite that way," said Smith. He cast a glance toward his house, and scratched his graying hair.

"Yeah, I guess not…"

The girl was coming back; Barr made his escape before her proud papa could corner him to show off more of her undoubted skills.

Barr didn't need directions to Iris's farm, *the Tamarack place* after her husband's family name; he'd checked it out, if from groundsense distance, some of the other times he'd found Lily to be visiting her cousins. He was fairly sure Iris would still recognize him, even after almost fifteen years. Lakewalkers aged more slowly than farmers, not to mention farm wives. For a moment, he regretted the recent loss of his maybe-disguising beard. Whether Iris would still hold a grudge against her sister's seducer was a question he'd never tested. He'd never seen her mistreat Lily, anyway, though Barr had to grant his stretches of observation had been brief.

There was no handy cover overlooking the Tamarack place, but the core buildings were close to the road. Barr stopped Briar in the speckled shade of a big elm tree flanking the farm lane, opening his perceptions wide. This farm was busy with life: chickens, cows, sheep, goats, horses, dogs, cats, all easily sensed and dismissed. A man and, yes, a boy were in the barn. Another three adults and what he guessed might be a couple of toddlers were at the back of the house, likely the kitchen. More youngsters upstairs, but not the sole one he sought.

He bit his lip and tried running through the inventory of humans once more, sorting out Masons from Tamaracks as best he could. Five or six each, maybe? Still no Lily. Two years older might have changed her, but not out of all recognition, not to him. That Lakewalker tinge should still color her. Maybe she'd been sent on an errand—not toward the village, or Barr would have passed her, but, say, up to the woods on the hill behind to gather fiddlehead ferns and other spring greens? A likely task to set a nimble-fingered youngster to, this time of year. Should he ride a pattern around the perimeter of the place?

As he mulled, the man and the boy came riding out of the barn on a horse and a pony respectively. Barr hesitated a little too long to pretend he was just riding by; the man spotted him and pressed his horse forward, pulling up by Barr's side. The searching look he treated Barr to was not quite what he was used to receiving from farmers, if still nothing warm. Not wary suspicion, but...anxiety?

The boy followed, staring more openly. "Uncle Jay!" he whispered. "Ain't that a Lakewalker?"

Thus pegging the man as Jay Tamarack, and the boy as Lily's next-down sibling—half-brother—Reeve, yes. Around twelve years old. Edjer had been what, nine? Ten? Barr touched his hand to his temple and tried a tentative, "Aye. How de'."

"You patrolling?" asked Jay, and then, oddly eager, "Is your patrol around?"

"Not at present. I'm just passing through. Heading home to Pearl Riffle." In which case he should be riding east from the crossroads, not west to this place, Barr belatedly realized, but the man didn't seem to notice.

"Which way did you come from?"

"Down the north road."

"In the past, what, two days I guess, did you chance to pass a girl about fourteen riding a little gray gelding?" He peered at Barr. "Hair about your color but a shade lighter, blue eyes."

Barr kept his hand from reaching back to touch the sandy-blond braid at his nape, bound by the cord with the shark teeth on it, souvenir of his long-ago trip to the sea. "Can't say as I have. But I only turned onto the north cross-road this morning, about six miles up from the Corner. I was on the patroller trails before then."

The man rubbed his forehead. "Oh, yeah, the trails, too. Not just the roads. This is a nightmare." He turned to the boy. "Reeve, ride on to your place, check it again. And anywhere around it where you kids hide to duck chores. Then the neighbors. Then anywhere else you can think of."

"I did that *yesterday*."

"She might have come back. If not here, that's still the most likely place for her to den up. Go on, git."

"Yeah, yeah," the boy sighed, kicking his pony into a trot.

"You folks missing a youngster?" Barr said, as neutrally as he could manage.

"My niece." Jay nodded. "There was a, a bad situation. We think she must have run off, on account of her taking her things and Moon. Though we did check down the wells, yesterday, both of them, here and there. There at her family's house that burned last month, I should say. I didn't think that likely, but you never know, and poor Fid insisted. Her pa. I'd say he's fit to be tied, except he already sort of is, with his hands so hurt."

Barr concealed a shudder. *Wells.* Yes, farmer children did accidentally fall and drown in wells, time to time. And sometimes not so accidentally... He considered the distance between a laughing roll in the hay on a bright summer afternoon, and probing a dark well for a young body, finding it oddly foreshortened.

Swallowing hard, Barr tried, "You know, I'm not in a hurry. I could lend you some help in your hunt for a bit, if you wanted me."

The man's lips parted in surprise, then a hesitant sort of thrill. "You Lakewalkers—you do find things. Blight bogles, they say."

"Malices—blight bogles, as you call 'em—are hard to miss, once you get anywhere near. Their blight looks like a forest fire touched down. And they stay put, through their first molt or three, anyway. One little farmer girl would be more skittery." He was briefly torn between promising nothing he did not know he could deliver, and selling himself like a river merchant, then realized it had better be the latter. "But yes. I'm a good hunter." The number of malice kills he could boast by now was not exactly relevant to the present problem. Explaining his groundsense range would be more to the point, but then he'd likely have to stop and explain groundsense. "I'd need more information to guess where to start, though." With a two, three day lead, mounted, Lily could be fifty miles down the road by now. But which road?

The worst thing he could do was pick the wrong direction to start out, and he only stood one chance in four of getting it right by guess.

"Come in, come in, then." Jay Tamarack turned his horse and gestured Barr ahead of him into the lane. "Fid would be so relieved. And Bell too, I imagine."

Wait, what? "No... I shouldn't trespass."

"You're *invited*." Jay gestured harder.

Oh, blight. It was obvious the secret of Lily's non-Mason-ness could not be generally known to the rest of her family. *Though Bell knows. And Iris.* So if they all three kept their heads, and their mouths shut... Leaving wells aside, Barr's imagination could provide a long list of lethal hazards a young woman might encounter, alone on the roads. He expected everyone else's could, too. The choice wasn't happy, but it was plain. Apprehensively, Barr let himself be shepherded onto the lane.

Jay Tamarack led him around to the back of the house, where they tied their horses. Barr gulped and followed him up the stoop and into the kitchen. It was a long room running the width of the house, with a fireplace and a new-style iron cookstove on one end, and a big table lined with benches to feed a crowd on the other. The morning's bread loaves, still warm and yeasty-smelling, stood in rows on a shelf below a back window.

Two women were at work chopping vegetables and topping up a soup kettle. A man occupying an end chair by the table, his arms and hands bandaged, gingerly balanced a toddler on his lap and kept it distracted with bread bits. Another child clumsily bashed a wooden horse and blocks around at his feet. All three grownups looked up at their entry, but only two reacted.

Bell's faded blue eyes widened in shock as she took Barr in. She was a little taller, a little thinner, than the girl he'd once known, her hair darkened to a drab tawny knot at her nape. Her ground was profoundly changed, shot through with recent stress and grief. Pregnant, yes, about four months gone, thickening at the waist under her apron. The bright new life within her seemed healthy enough, though.

Iris had always been taller than her younger sister, brown-haired to her blond, cautious to her boldness. More mature, not much change there; drained by fewer pregnancies. It took her a longer moment to recognize Barr, and that mostly from following her sister's jerk and stare. She recoiled, then stepped forward protectively.

"You!" cried Bell, cutting across Barr's vague opening mumble as he strove to act as if they'd never met before. "Did you take Lily?"

"What? No!"

"Bell—!" said Jay, startled by this out-of-the-blue accusation. Barr hoped he'd put it down to his sister-in-law's distraught state of mind.

"Did you bring her back?" Iris said more urgently.

"Not yet," Barr said. He gestured at Iris's husband, and hastily filled in, "I just met this fellow out on the road, where he stopped me and asked if I'd seen a missing girl, since I'd come down the north crossroad this morning. Which I was sorry to say I had not, but since I'm not on a patrol, I thought I could pause for a bit and help you all to look." He went on steadily, trying to recover the play-act if they wanted it, "Name's Barr, of Tent Foxbrush out of Pearl Riffle Camp, down on the Grace River. And you folks might be...?" He blinked, trying to convey his good intention.

Iris at least caught on. She grasped her sister's arm rather hard as Bell started forward; Barr hoped the kitchen knife clutched in her hand was merely forgotten. "That's right kindly of you, Lakewalker," Iris got out through only slightly gritted teeth. "What do you think you could do?"

Barr feigned a shrug. "Ride farther, look faster. Extend the range of the search." He added, "I'm thinking, though, that not all the powers at my command will do a mite of good if I'm not looking in the right direction. I was hoping we might sit down and try to work out which one that would be." He added prudently, "And then I could be on my way." *No, see, I'm not trying to burn down your life... Again.*

Fid put down the toddler and rose a bit painfully from his seat. He limped over to Barr with a hoping look on his face that was downright alarming. "Really? You would do that, lad?"

We're the same age, Fid. Best not to point that out.

"I'm Fid Mason, Lily's papa, by the way," he added, extending a bandaged hand, then venting a rueful laugh as if to apologize for his incapacity and letting it drop.

Barr ducked his head in acknowledgment of it all. "How de' y' do, sir." Not well, Barr could see; the burns under those bandages were deep and ugly, oozing with inflammation.

Thinking that he'd better not reveal his prior conversation with the smith, nor that this visit wasn't by chance, Barr then plunged the room into an abrupt and unintended silence by asking the next obvious question: "Why d'you suppose the girl ran off, does anyone know?"

Lots of set jaws: Bell angry, Fid distressed, Jay glum, Iris closed like a river mussel. Or she would be, if Barr couldn't read all their grounds like a patrol report page.

Barr pressed on: "Because if I knew why, it would be the first step in guessing where to."

Jay said, "At first we thought she'd hole in with a friend or a neighbor till she got over her mad, or hide out back home, but we've not found her in any of those places so far."

"You folks will be better at covering all your local patch," Barr allowed. "But if she picked a direction and kept on going, I've a better chance of catching up to her. So which way?" And, a little frustrated, "Doesn't anyone talk to the girl? Can't you tell me anything at all about how she thinks?"

Bell crossed her arms tight and glowered at the floor. "She's a liar," she muttered.

"Now, Bell, we can't know that," said Jay, in a tone of wearied placation.

"Not anymore, for sure," said Iris grimly. Since little Edjer had gone into the ground, Barr guessed she meant, and any chance of recanting his testimony buried with him. Bell flinched. Iris set an apologetic arm around her sister's shoulders.

After a glance at his wife, Fid picked his words carefully. "Lily was accused of not telling the truth about something, and took it in bad part. Rode off in a huff, I daresay."

He made it sound like some youthful fib, not the mortal mess Barr knew it to be.

"Or rode off guilty and ashamed," grumbled Bell.

"And which was it?" said Barr.

Jay cast a glance at Iris, who said, "We just can't tell."

A Lakewalker could. Despite all his boundless duties, and the ritual of death he not just knew but hoped lay at the end of them, Barr was suddenly glad to be one. His hand brushed the unprimed bone knife concealed in its sheath at his side, his constant companion and final promise.

"She has a temper," Fid offered. "And never liked injustices."

"Who does?" said Jay.

This was getting circular, like a ring of reproach and concern with a Lily-shaped blank in the middle. *And you're part of that blind ring too, aren't you, patroller?* "All right," Barr sighed, "try this. Every away contains a toward. Did she ever talk of any place she dreamed of going? Some place she wanted to see? I mean, before all this blew up. Or did anyone talk to her of places to go, tell exciting stories?"

Jay scratched his head. "Well, everybody around here talks about the river. It's not only where I'd go, it's where I did go, when I was a youngster. Though I came back when

I'd got it out of my system." His mouth twisted up at his wife. "Plus there was this girl. That'll anchor your boat."

Iris's return lip-twitch suggested this was an old joke, without a sting.

Barr's ground survey, opening him uncomfortably to all the pain in the room, wasn't helping much. Everyone here was telling the truth as they knew it, and no one was telling him what he needed to know. He massaged his neck under his braid, steeling himself. "Miz Mason, Miz Tamarack, could I talk to you both private for a bit?"

The two sisters looked at each other; reluctantly, Bell nodded. "Come out to the front porch. Fid, keep an eye on the childers." Intervention would be needed soon, as a squabble was brewing at knee level over the wooden horse. "Keep them"—her voice caught—"away from the fireplace."

"Aye," said Fid, a twinge echoing through his ground at this last. He limped over to lower himself to the floor and mediate between the two chubby-fisted cousins.

"Jay, weren't you going to ride out?" said Iris.

"I'll fetch the Lakewalker a sack of grain to take along for his horse, first," said Jay. "Seems the least we can do. You feed him, too, before he goes, eh?" He departed out the back door as Iris led Barr and her sister through her house to the front.

Barr leaned against one porch post in the shade of its roof. Bell took the other, as if in mirror to him. Iris sat herself down on the step between, part guardian, part buffer, and turned toward Barr.

He took a breath. "First thing. I didn't ride by here on accident."

"I didn't think you did," murmured Bell darkly.

"I'd stopped in and talked to Smith back at the Corner. He told me about your barn and house, and Edjer." Barr took refuge from the impossible-to-encompass in formality. "I am sorry for your loss."

Bell curled in on herself as if around a knife wound. That lip movement might have been an attempt at a *Thank you.*

Barr's fingers fiddled again with his bone hilt, long-time consolation for any nerves or distress. People who knew him well, like Remo or Dag, would have spotted it for the sign it was right off. But here, his anxious spirit was safely cocooned in his audience's ignorance. "Smith also told me how Lily and Edjer accused each other of letting the fire start."

"We just can't know," Iris repeated, whether to Bell or Barr he wasn't sure.

Bell stared away over the sunlit field, but there was no light in her eyes. "She shouldn't have spoke ill of the dead. Anyhow."

Barr thought that if Bell had a year, or three, she might get over her grief for her lost child enough to be fair to the other one again. Or at least to forgive her. Although if Lily was actually the innocent party, he could see where *forgiveness* would be the most searing insult imaginable. And Lily didn't have three years to wait out this heart-storm, not at her fast-moving age.

"Did you get along all right with Lily? Before this?"

"She was an obedient child, most t' time," said Bell, a muscle twitching in her jaw. Iris nodded confirmation of this tepid praise.

"Ever tell her about me?"

Bell looked up sharply. "No!"

"Let it slip on accident?" His glance swept Iris as well, who shook her head.

"No." Bell's voice firmed up on this one. "It couldn't do her, nor Fid, nor anyone else any good by now. No." Her glance under her lashes suggested she would erase Barr from the whole world if she could; but erasing him from Lily's world would have to do.

"So this running away can't have to do with her finding out all sudden who she is?"

Bell shook her head. "I shouldn't think so."

"If she's inherited any of my Lakewalker powers, they should be starting to rise just about now. You see any sign? Or word?"

"No…" This denial sounded less certain. "But if so, her mother'd be the last person she'd tell. It's not like we clashed more than our fair share, mind. This's got nothing to do with her and me, but a whole lot to do with being fourteen. It's never a good age, for a girl."

Iris nodded wry confirmation. Remembering who-knew-what from their shared farmer girlhoods? Barr didn't have a farmer girlhood to draw on for insight, and wasn't sure how much of the notable and prolonged head-butting he'd done with his own Lakewalker parents could fill in. Maybe some…

And all this could be as true as both women thought it was, but he still needed a direction.

"Do you have any relatives or friends she knows about in other towns?" He did not add, *Or camps?* Lily might have two grandparents, a handful of aunts and uncles, and a clutch of young cousins in Pearl Riffle Camp, not to mention a passel of more remote tent-kin, but they could not enter into this calculation. He was part relieved, and part glumly thinking that at least it would be *something.* "Glassforge, Silver Shoals, Lumpton Market, anyplace smaller?"

"I suppose we must, but none we've ever visited nor kept in touch with," said Iris. "Our people came from south of the Grace, originally."

Which was true of nearly every farmer in Oleana, so not much help there. Maybe he really was going to have to ride back to the Corner and flip a coin.

Half-a-dozen more probing questions got Barr no further. How could these people have been with Lily all her life, yet know so little about her? It seemed too cruel a thing to ask out loud. Well, they were busy, absent gods knew, that was part of it. Farm life was work from sunup to sunset. And the lack of groundsense would make anyone seem blind. Barr sighed and let himself be led back to the kitchen for a hasty, if wholesome, meal.

Fid and the toddlers had disappeared upstairs, but the man came outside as Barr was stowing his gift rations in his saddlebags and tightening the girth. Barr eyed him sideways. Fid seemed the next most likely after Bell to have noticed any sign of Lily manifesting Lakewalker powers, but he was the last person Barr could ask.

Hesitantly, Fid shook out a wad of cloth to reveal a worn blouse. "I wondered if you could use something of Lily's. To find or recognize her."

Barr snorted. "Patrollers aren't scent hounds. It doesn't work like that." He frowned at the pathetic garment. "Though it might be good to have something to prove my tale. Because she isn't going to know me from a hole in the ground."

Fid nodded. "That had crossed my mind, too." He held out a letter, fastened with a wax seal. "If—when—you find her, give her this from me."

"Ah. Better thinking."

"How will you recognize her, then?" asked Fid.

"Besides her general description, groundsense. From, urm, seeing you and Bell. There's a family look." Which was true, if not in the way Barr implied. Barr took both proffered talismans, wrapping the letter in the blouse and stashing them in his saddlebag. Lily's name on the outside of the folded paper had been painstakingly but clumsily inked. "How are your arms and hands doing?"

Fid shrugged. "Burns are slow to heal."

No lie. The man was in throbbing pain even yet. "I could do a spot of patroller field aid on them, before I go. If you like."

Fid looked surprised. "I thought Lakewalkers weren't supposed to share their healing magic with farmers."

Groundwork, not magic. Barr did not bother trying to correct the common miswording. "Yeah, well, Lakewalkers do a lot of things they aren't supposed to do. Turns out."

"I...yes, then. Please. Seems worth trying."

A touch warily, Fid took a seat on the stoop, and Barr knelt next to him. He cradled first one arm and then the other in his hands, laying in the simplest possible ground reinforcement to fight infection and speed healing. He wasn't up to fancy groundwork like Dag, or Dag's ground-setter kinsman Arkady Redwing, whose healing work went, it sometimes seemed, beyond magic to miracle. But Barr could do his share, and had, many times out on patrol.

Simple, but not weak. He poured out all the strength he could spare, which had grown over the years to be far more than his callow, shallow younger self could ever have mustered, or even imagined. As Dag had trained him, he took care to allow the ground backflow that undercut inadvertent beguilement, though it made him flinch. The last thing he wanted was Fid fixating on him, becoming obsessed, for good or ill. Though some stray spill of amity might do no harm...

Fid looked nonplussed as he gingerly patted his bandages. "Feels warm. But not bad. Like the opposite of fever."

"You'll want to change out those bandages often, for clean and dry."

"We been doin' that regular already, yes."

Barr grunted to his feet. Like a diligent host, Fid rose after him, watching him as he mounted up.

"Any last thoughts on which way?" Barr asked.

Fid shook his head. "All I can guess is that she'll be hurtin'. And angry. Not the best state of mind for thinking straight."

"So I observed," said Barr dryly.

Fid took his meaning without effort. "Aye." He swallowed, lifting his chin. "If you can't find her...stop back and let us know that as well, can you?"

"I promise you, I will search with everything in my powers." The limits of which Barr had not tested lately. That might be about to change.

He gave Fid a vague salute, much as he might bid farewell to a camp friend when starting out on a patrol, and reined his horse back to the road.

BARR SAT ATOP Briar at the Hackberry Corner crossroads and flipped a coin, over and over. It was a trick that worked sometimes to flush out his opinions from the back of his own head, but none of its outcomes here either drew or deterred him. And he tried them all, twice.

A cautious voice interrupted his tail-chasing: "You all right, Mister Lakewalker?"

He glanced down in surprise to see Meggie, the smith's daughter, minus her leather apron and with a basket on her arm, regarding him with the air of someone studying a sick, strange animal.

"Thank you, Miss Smith, I'm..." He looked down at her again. For a Lakewalker, Barr was pretty well-versed in guessing farmer ages. "Aren't you about as old as Lily Mason?"

A wary nod.

"Are you friends?"

"Some..."

"Have you heard that she's run off from her home?"

Nod. "Her brother Reeve came around looking for her."

"Her family's asked me to help hunt for her."

"Oh, I see." She considered this gravely. "What if she don't want to be found?"

Barr felt as if he'd just rolled the winning number at dice. He smiled blindingly and dismounted, preparing to pour out all the charm he possessed. She blinked and backed up a step. "No one in her family could guess which way she'd gone; but I'm thinking maybe she'd have been more open with a friend. Miss Smith, might you be so kind as to spare me a moment of talk?"

Not giving her a chance to refuse, he took her arm and steered her to the bench beside the village well at the center of the square, settling them both down in the noon sun. She hitched away, but didn't spring up and run. It would do for a start.

"I really don't know anything either," she said. "Lily didn't talk to me before she lit out. I guess she wasn't much talking to anyone by then."

Barr nodded. "I've been thinking it through. She didn't take more than what food and fodder her horse could carry, along with herself, and I gather she didn't have much coin. Only enough for a few days' ride." Not like the hundreds of miles an experienced patroller expected to cover between rests. "She'll have to stop and regroup, somehow. Find work, maybe. D'you think she'd go for a hired girl?" Which would only give him, absent gods, about ten thousand farms at which to ask after her. In any direction.

Meggie, unexpectedly, scoffed. "Not likely, not Lily. That's the work she's been doing all her life. Comes with being oldest, which I'm glad I'm not. Fetch and carry at the word of the farmwife, do the chores and mind the children? I'm not saying she'd starve first, or me neither, but there's better work out there if you're going."

"But not on a farm. In a town?"

A deflecting shoulder-hitch, but with that flicker of assent in her ground, Barr didn't have to bully her into revelations.

"Which town d'you think she'd favor? A big river crossing like Silver Shoals, or Lumpton Market to the north, or Glassforge, east?"

A bigger flicker. "Hah. If I were running away, I'd pick Glassforge in a heartbeat. They say they're doing ironwork around there that makes a village smithy look no-how. Water-powered hammers! But Lily ain't me. Not so fond of fire." A pensive look crossed her face. "'Specially not now, I expect."

"Mm," Barr agreed. "So what does she like?"

"Horses," said Meggie, with some certainty. "She sure loves her Moon. I'd swear he loves her right back. You'd think they talked to each other in people. I shod him, last time. Good manners."

That…did not narrow it down. Half the girls that age that Barr had ever met, Lakewalker or farmer, were horse-mad. "Anything else?"

"She likes the woods, and being outside."

That did not point to a town, either. Still less a specific town.

"Though you can't live in the woods," Meggie mused. "…Well, I suppose you Lakewalkers do."

"For all we spend more time patrolling than in camp, the trail isn't home, no." He frowned. "So what about the river? She ever talk about it?"

Meggie wrinkled her nose. "River's where boys run off to if they've made too much trouble at home, and girls if they're ruined. Lily ain't ruined, just mad."

Putting Barr all too swiftly in mind of the bed boats, enterprises that he'd never thought of as a *hazard*, before. *Er.*

"Not that being ruined wouldn't make you mad, too, on top of it," Meggie went on thoughtfully.

Barr pictured Bell, and barely kept himself from grunting glum assent. "Well, thank you for your time, Miss Smith."

She rose with him. "Was I any help?"

"Mm, maybe. I'll find out as I go, I expect."

"Lily," she began, then stopped.

Barr raised his brows at her. "Hm?"

She frowned at her feet. "She might not want to come back. Then what?"

"We'll burn that bridge when we come to it, I guess." He meant it for a joke, but she shot him a startled look, not altogether disapproving, and he wondered if he might have said more than he meant. Or meant to.

Meggie hoisted her basket and went on her way, and Barr returned to Briar, waiting patiently, and mounted up once more. He let out a long, uncertain breath, then turned east.

He'd just have to keep asking along the way if anyone had seen Lily. If someone had, he could press ahead with speed and certainty. If he picked up no farmer-girl spoor by the time he reached Glassforge, he'd need to turn around and start retracing his steps. Conscripting the entire Pearl Riffle patrol cadre to keep a spare eye out for her as they quartered the countryside hunting for new-hatched malices was…very much a last resort, for all it would vastly increase his coverage.

He wondered if bringing Lily back safe would go some way to make up to Bell for the hurt he'd dealt her, all those years ago, or if it was just plain stupid to hanker for forgiveness. Maybe so. Doing this for Lily, well, that made more sense. Though it didn't sound as though she'd be happy with his efforts, either. *You're a blighted patroller, Barr. Riding forever for no reward is what you do. Get on with it.*

The sun seemed to be racing across the sky. He put his back to it, and his heels to Briar's sides, urging her into that long-legged patrol jog that ate the miles.

BARR DIDN'T GUESS that Lily was likely to stop her journey within a day's ride of her home, so he concentrated that afternoon on speed, not side-casts. Riding at double patrol pace, with his groundsense stretched to its widest just in case, proved exhausting by the time dusk overtook him well east of Hackberry Corner. He picked an empty old campsite a few paces off the road that had a glimmering creek running by it, then set to the calming routine of unsaddling and tending to his mount.

He was grateful for Jay Tamarack's gift of grain, a hearty mixture of oats and dried shelled corn, that would cut the time Briar would need to spend grazing. He curried her down—she was still shedding clouds of winter hairs— checked her legs for botfly eggs, ears and stern for any new parasites, and tended to her hooves. Then he took the opportunity to lead her to a chest- and barrel-deep pool down the stream and wash both her and himself, which she seemed to enjoy. They splashed each other vigorously.

The foal within her was still doing fine. Briar was of the hardiest of Luthlian patrol stock, with a leg length to match his own, bred up to the best stallion his exchange camp had boasted. She and her offspring were at once part payment for his late labors, and a gift of fresh bloodlines to the herd of his own camp. He'd been taking the thousand-mile-trek home in gentle stages for the past two months, but it seemed she'd be well up to the challenge of his new hunt.

No malice sign sensed today, but he didn't expect any this close to the roads that both farmers and Lakewalkers shared. Such routes got checked too often, as few Lakewalkers, patroller or camp-folk, went anywhere without habitually keeping their extra sense alert much as he just had today. Except in farmer towns; too much painful noise there. Any patrol working this area would be up beyond the rolling hills, checking hidden and difficult patches seldom visited.

He dried and dressed again, then munched on a portion of the cold food from the Tamarack farm that would save him as much time as it saved Briar. He needed neither the light nor, absent gods knew, the heat in this muggy spring evening, but he nonetheless busied himself making a tiny campfire. He set his steel hunting knife to the flame, then, thoughtfully, dug Fid's letter out of his saddlebag.

The hot blade, held briefly to the backside of the letter, was enough to loosen the wax seal without breaking it. He gently folded the paper open to the crabbed writing inside. Not hardly even the most dodgy thing he'd ever done, but there was honest need, here. He wasn't about to risk handing Lily what might be a piece of poison, all unaware.

The stilted wording that he slowly made out was... heartbreaking, really. Assurance that this Lakewalker fellow Barr was sent for her. A plea to return home, an affirmation that her father believed her side—which seemed late off the mark, frankly—an entreaty for merciful understanding of her mother's distress, a prediction that all would be well again in time, just give it time. Which seemed to Barr more an expression of Fid's hope than a likely event, and he wondered if it would seem that way to Lily, too. Barr could sense how the love that shone between the awkward lines, so obvious to his own eyes, might not be so plain to her anger-clouded ones.

No accusations of bastardy, certainly. No renewed reproach. No obvious pit-traps dug around Barr's task of returning her home. Which was all he needed to know. He refolded the letter and applied his knife again to reseal it, wrapping it up carefully to put away once more.

By LATE THE next morning, Barr was growing anxious about his direction. Half-a-dozen pauses to query people who might have been keeping watch on the road netted nothing. But then, as he was passing through a straggling hamlet, his eye was caught by a sign on the gate of a shabby clapboard house with bright flowers set in pots around its porch. *Rooms and meals for decent travelers. Ask inside.* He thought Lily's eye might have been caught, too.

And so it turned out. The widow who earned a little coin on this roadside venture remembered the blond girl with the neat gray gelding very well, on what Barr calculated could have been the first or second night of her flight. She was going to Glassforge, she'd said, to visit an aunt, and maybe find work as a hired girl. She'd given the name of Rue, turning her hand to helping with chores in return for a markdown on her board, working courteously and with unusual thoroughness. If not very cheerfully; the girl'd been on the quiet side, really. The widow hoped the patroller fellow, tasked with delivering an urgent message for her to turn around and come home on account of her mother falling ill, would find her soon.

Proving Barr as glib as evolving fibs as…a fourteen-year-old girl, right, he reflected moodily as he rode on. Or maybe it was in the blood? *Let's not think about that.* Not that Lily couldn't dart off in some other direction at any crossroad, but he pressed eastward with renewed hope and speed.

Either one alone might not have been memorable, but along his afternoon's ride he found the combination of the girl and the gray gelding had been noted twice more. So far so good. He grew more confident about Glassforge, although finding Lily in that busy town was going to be a groundsense nightmare. *I've stood as much and more before,* he told himself sternly. *No whining from the pillion seat.*

THE NEXT DAY, a few miles short of where his easterly track crossed the big north-south straight road that ran from the Grace River up through Glassforge, Barr found some luck at last. He sat up in his saddle and reined in his horse as an approaching woman, clad and armed as a Lakewalker patroller, did the same. She was closely trailed by, yes, a farmer youth wearing one of the new-fangled groundshields.

The design of the pendant around his neck was the standard one that Dag and Arkady had worked out some years ago, dense groundwork anchored in a walnut inside its shell, contained in a little net bag hung on a cord. It masked that painful, uncontrolled farmer flare to next to nothing, making the wearer not only tolerable to—and, less touted, protected from—Lakewalkers, but shielded from the much stronger mind-invasion of malices. And, thus, potential help instead of pure risk on a patrol. Barr had partnered and helped train up some of the first farmer volunteers himself, in the early stages down at Pearl Riffle. This lad was not one Barr recognized, though.

Barr and the patroller woman, who looked to be about fifty, exchanged salutes across their saddlebows. The farmer lad watched with strong interest.

"How de', ma'am," Barr began. "I'm doing a favor for a farmer friend, a ways west of here." And what a mark of progress it was that this statement sounded plausible, though the *friend* part was stretching it. "The daughter of the house ran off, and I said I'd help find her. Have you chanced across a girl of about fourteen, blond, riding a choice little gray gelding? Probably heading up to Glassforge." Although by Barr's estimate, she should have reached the town yesterday. "Her name's Lily, but she might be calling herself Rue." Or any number of other tales; Barr, collecting them in her wake, was becoming loth to underestimate Lily's inventiveness.

The patroller woman's brows climbed. She exchanged a look with her lad.

"We saw a blond girl riding a pretty gray when we were coming up the old straight road earlier this morning, but she wasn't going north. She passed us going south. We turned off here soon after, so I don't know where she went beyond that. But she wasn't a farmer."

"What?" said Barr.

"Young Lakewalker with really bad ground control, I thought, maybe upset. Not from our camp. I called after her, asking if she needed help, but she just shot this scared look over her shoulder and set her horse into a canter. I was a little concerned, but we had a courier route to complete." She nodded to the lad. "I'm teaching it to Stocker."

Stocker ducked his head shyly to Barr.

"That's a good making on that groundshield," Barr observed kindly. "Is it Maker Verel's work, out of Pearl Riffle? It feels familiar."

"Close. You've a shrewd eye." The woman grinned. "Verel trained our knife maker at Muskrat Slough Camp how to do it."

Muskrat Slough's patrol territory bordered that of Pearl Riffle on the northeast; they hadn't been participating in the new trial at the time Barr had left for Luthlia. So, the work was spreading, much as Dag and Arkady had hoped, picked up from camp to camp. It didn't sound as if any lurid mishaps had undercut the effort yet, either, though there were bound to be hitches sometime.

"I'm Astrie Graygoose of Muskrat Slough, by the way, and this is my apprentice. He's been training for half a year, so far."

"I hope to be let go on a real patrol, soon," Stocker confided to Barr.

Without groundsense, farmer-patrollers couldn't help scan for malices on the pattern-sweeps, but there was plenty of support work to be done for a moving patrol. Arkady had been encouraging patrol leaders to keep careful records, to try and see if farmer helpers made a discernible difference in a patrol's speed and efficiency, not just ease. Dag, and Barr with him, thought the real value was in bringing farmers into patroller methods so they could go home again and tell accurate stories, bridging the dangerous gulf of communication between the two peoples. Because as more farmers moved north into what had once been exclusively Lakewalker territories, the chance—no, the certainty—of bad malice attacks like the one near Glassforge a dozen years back, or that lethal break-out over in Raintree that had wiped out an entire village, most of a camp, and made a mess of hundreds of square miles of territory, were bound to increase.

Barr touched his temple. "I'm Barr of Tent Foxbrush, down at Pearl Riffle. Been away to Luthlia, just on my way home."

Barr expected the woman to be impressed by his distant exchange patrol, and indeed her eyes widened. But instead she gasped, "Barr of Pearl Riffle? I've heard of you! Maker Verel talked all about you!"

Barr cringed. The Pearl Riffle medicine maker, after all, had known him since his birth, and been a close witness to his erratic youth, patching him up any number of times. "Oh?" he said warily.

"He said you were involved in that nasty episode south of the Grace off the Tripoint Trace, a few years back. Is it true that malice made mud-men that could *fly?*"

Malices, once they reached full-enough powers, could mold distorted half-intelligent slaves out of animals, which

Lakewalkers dubbed all too descriptively *mud-men*. The process was gut-wrenching, and so were the results. "Yep, evil thing hatched out in the mouth of a bat cavern, up in those limestone hills. Must have been like being born into a banquet. It had *millions* of the little critters to ground-rip for power, right to hand." Ordinary bats still gave Barr a twinge. "It made itself a crew of big ones, about the size of a dog. Huge wings on 'em. A pack of them could get together and lift a man right out of his saddle." *Yeah, ask me how I know this. Better still, don't.* The Trace malice's mud-bats were still the stuff of Barr's nightmares.

Both the patroller and her farmer apprentice looked awestruck.

Barr cut across mouths opening with more questions. He was usually good for a long patroller gossip, though preferably over farmer beer, but not today. He half-saluted again. "Well. I'd best be on my way, or my quarry will be out of range again. Thank you muchly for your lead."

"Fare safe," Astrie said, letting him go with obvious reluctance. "I hope you find that girl."

"So do I, ma'am."

As Barr rode away, he could hear the farmer lad whispering fiercely, "D'you think he was telling the truth about the flying malice? Or was that a tall tale?"

"*Oh* yes," replied the courier, who would know. The boy stared agog back over his shoulder. Barr set his jaw and pushed on.

HE PAUSED FOR a long moment at the junction with the old straight road, mulling. It wasn't as if Lily could be the only blond girl with a gray nag in all of Oleana, and the worry that he might have been chasing the wrong fox for several days was maddening. Glassforge drew him, not least for the memory of a certain very comfortable inn that gave free rooms to patrollers, which would make a dandy base for his search of the town.

But no. If he tried, he could likely overtake the girl that the patroller woman had seen in a few hours, at least if she stayed within half a mile of the road. If she was the wrong one, he could still double back to Glassforge. If he went to Glassforge first, the girl would pass beyond hope of his catching her for sure. He turned Briar south and chirped her into a trot.

The sun was dipping below the trees to the west when a flicker off the road to his left stopped his breath, and Briar. They were passing a stretch of steeper wooded hills, rugged and unfarmed. A shallow creek draining them crossed the road, so modest it didn't even rate a bridge, just a splashing ford. About a quarter mile up it, a single person lurked, and, yes, a single horse.

He tried to quell his hope, to persuade himself that the spiky, flaring ground he felt was unfamiliar. It was certainly not the same as the one he'd last burned into his memory two years ago, but then, his own probably wasn't, either. A person grew, and their ground grew with them. *The underlying truth of the world,* Maker Arkady had once described ground, so how could it not?

Yeah. We've arrived. He turned Briar into the creek, letting her pick her way slowly over the stones. He'd had plenty of time on his ride to rehearse how the blight he was going to present himself to Lily, and none of the scenes exactly matched this one. He'd figured to find her in some peopled place and study her from a distance, first. Make his approach casual, polite and unalarming. For starters, a man sneaking up on a girl alone in the woods could be misunderstood in so many awkward ways it would be funny, except it wasn't. *Well, then, don't sneak. Make noise.* Briar's hooves were doing a fair job at that, scraping and splashing.

Barr let his groundsense ease from its full stretch, going loose and relaxed. He could sense her, and get a sense of her, before she saw him, at least.

Except he hadn't expected to be sensed back.

He flinched at her sudden recoil and panic. By the time her simple campsite, tucked into an opening in the underbrush by the creek side, came into the view of his eyes, she was on her feet and had darted behind her unsaddled horse, gripping its mane as if to vault aboard and flee. Moon's head, too, was up, eyes wide and nostrils flaring.

Oh, dear, that horse. Every bit as pretty as described: salt-and-pepper mane and tail, near-white coat blending to dapples over the haunches like some fancy brocade cloth,

and trim gray legs and hooves. In height, just on the bor-
derline of a pony and a horse, as his mistress was on the
cusp between girl and woman, but slim-built, not a shaggy
barrel-on-legs.

And Barr had never seen a more beguiled animal in his
life. From nose to tail, downright *besotted*. Not that the feelings weren't returned in full, he expected. Moon's legs were
planted foursquare in a defensive posture, neck bent and
head lowered toward Barr, ears back, as if ready to fend off
a catamount from a foal.

The tow-headed girl sheltered behind this restive bul-
wark had grown taller than Barr had pictured, also in that
slim-built style just before the fullness of a woman's body
overtook her. It was probably chance, or travel practicality,
that her pale hair was drawn back in a thick braid at her
nape nearly identical to Barr's own. Minus the souvenir
shark teeth. Bright blue eyes, now narrowed in anger and
fear. Long-fingered hands, promising still more growth to
come, one clutching a fistful of mane, the other a drawn belt-
knife. Ordinary blouse, limp and dirty with the day's sweat
and heat, riding trousers that might be a brother's or her
own, good leather boots just now jammed over bare feet in
her scramble up, still unfastened.

And an upset, unguarded ground that beat on him, at
this range, like a river torrent.

He wondered briefly when, over the years, he had so
thoroughly convinced himself that Lily would grow to her
farmer side as to not even entertain the notion she'd throw

not just Lakewalker, but *strongly* Lakewalker. And why? To help steel himself to keep his distance, as her mother had demanded? Or because she wouldn't be his problem, then?

Well, looks like she's my problem now. In so many ways.

Barr pulled his own ground in, drew breath through his teeth, stretched his lips in a smile that he suspected looked horribly false, and touched his temple in the same polite salute he'd lately offered his patroller informant. Keeping his voice as even as he could, he began with what he hoped would be the most immediate possible reassurance: "Miss Lily Mason? My name is Barr Foxbrush, and your family back in Hackberry Corner asked me to find you. Your friend Meggie Smith guessed you might have come this way. I have a letter for you from your papa Fid." There. All his authentication out on the table at once. And if it wasn't enough, he was in trouble.

Her tension didn't ease. "My mother would never deal with a Lakewalker."

She did once, Barr did not say. "She wasn't keen on it, but you threw your family into something of a tizzy, disappearing like that without a word or a note. And your papa couldn't chase you on account of his burns, though I got the notion he would've if he'd 'a could."

Slowly, Barr dismounted, but had the wits not to start toward her yet. This was trickier than persuading a wild animal to come to his hand with food. What in the wide green world would she consider nourishment? True, he had more direct methods at his command for persuading farmer girls, *ouch*, and he'd thought he might be forced to use them if he had trouble getting her turned back toward her home, but he'd never imagined she'd be able to *see them coming*.

"Do, um, I take from this that you've never dealt with a Lakewalker either?"

She shook her head. "I seen a patrol going down the west road a time or two. I took to the hedge."

That wouldn't have hidden you from them. "Well, we're not scary folks."

Her glower over her horse's withers denied this assertion in the strongest way. "Isn't it true you chop up your dead to make magic knives of their bones?"

He could hardly say *no*, but *yes* seemed fraught with pitfalls. "It's a solemn ritual. Part of our burial rites. Not whatever pig butchery you're picturing." Though harvesting thigh bones was unavoidably messy, true, and he'd helped in the process more than once. A grim and sad task, and this was not the time to go into those details. The emergency to hand was Lily's out-of-control ground and groundsense.

Blight it, there had been *no sign* of such a development in her two years ago. Or he'd have taken steps, though he'd no idea what kind. Not gone off to Luthlia, maybe, or at the very least, detailed a trusted patroller friend to keep an eye on his behalf. And how sad was it that he could not call to mind more than one patroller friend he trusted that much? Remo at least knew about Lily, and would have had the wits to check on her if Barr hadn't come back, but Remo had long since transferred north to Hickory Lake Camp, and was happy there, or as happy as Remo ever got. String-bound to a nice girl, too, as Barr's parents frequently pointed out, with meaningful looks his way.

Which jogged his recall of his own rather late and abrupt blooming into his full powers, and the really *annoying* anxiety on the part of his tent-kin that had preceded it. *I should have remembered that.*

He leaned against Briar's shoulder; she drooped her ears and leaned back, blowing out her breath in a placid huff. He tried feeding a little of her calm toward Moon, whose ears unflattened and flicked, though the gelding kept a wary eye on the intruders.

Which promptly rebounded, as Lily jerked up and cried, "What are you doing to my horse?"

Barr stayed still and let his brows rise; kept his voice level. "You feel that, did you? That was a touch of Lakewalker groundwork."

By her look of outrage, the coin was not dropping for her. Barr sighed and added explicitly, "Which you could not have felt unless you had Lakewalker blood yourself. You ever suspect that?"

"*What...?!*"

No, evidently. Or she might have been way more curious about patrollers passing through Hackberry Corner. Barr guessed any talk of Lakewalkers was strongly discouraged around the Mason house, so at this point Lily likely knew pretty much nothing about what was happening inside her. *Argh.*

Growing up in a Lakewalker camp, Barr had been as ground-blind as any other child, but he'd had people all around him with groundsense who knew what to do with it, talked about it, did tricks with it, instructed him in what to expect—well, apart from his one older brother who'd done his cackling best to fill Barr's young head with terrifying fables, for which Barr had still not entirely forgiven him. The rest of his kin had looked forward to and applauded any little sign of his power's advent. What if all those sputtering first reports from his new sense had possessed no explanation? Would he have thought himself going mad?

Had Lily?

"That's not possible!" gasped Lily. "Lakewalkers are evil sorcerers!"

Barr rubbed the back of his neck, trying to look as hangdog and unthreatening as possible, and offered, "Oh, come on, do I look like an evil sorcerer to you?" Which...might not be as clever a ploy as it seemed at first blush, because what if she said *Yes!*

She did look as though she was thinking about it. Embarrassingly hard. But what she finally came up with was, "How could I possibly have Lakewalker blood?"

"Got a Lakewalker somewhere up your family tree, I expect, maybe on more than one side. Two lines cross, and then sometimes you get a throwback." Barr tried to make it sound as if distant and unremembered umpty-great grandparents were at fault. It did happen that way, time to time. This reflection suddenly made him wonder about Bluebell's ancestry, but that was a curiosity for some less-fraught moment.

Barr went on, invitingly, "The last, what, half-year, year, must have been really confusing for you, then. Worse'n wisdom teeth, when your groundsense comes in. All those flickers in your mind that don't seem to be coming from anywhere. And all that blare leaking from unshielded people. Maybe disturbing for them, too, when you start reading their feelings, and have no way of getting away from 'em, and they don't understand why you're suddenly saying all those strange things."

Lily slipped her knife back into its sheath, a hopeful sign, but only to clutch Moon's mane tighter in both hands. "I never said anything. To anyone."

"Lonely, too, then, sounds like," Barr tossed out, lure-like.

He hadn't expected a blighted emotional *shark* to lunge for it. Her mouth crumpled up and she dropped to her knees with a choke, swiftly muffled as she caught her face in her hands. Moon turned and lowered his nose to snuffle her hair in a concerned fashion. She switched over to burying her bit-back sobs in his silky neck.

Barr gnawed his knuckle, uncertain whether to advance or retreat. The open distress in her made him nigh frantic, because unshielded emotions were contagious, as many a patrol leader had needed to deal firmly with. He finally dropped Briar's reins, trod over, and lowered himself cross-legged an arm's reach from her. When her shakes trailed off, which didn't take as long as it felt like, he tentatively offered her a bracing pat on the shoulder. He might have done the same to a fellow patroller having a breakdown, nothing paternal there at all, necessarily. She recoiled much less, this time. Good? He caught his hands together in his lap to prevent mishaps. Inadvertent hugs, for example, which he sensed would be inadvisable.

She rubbed her eyes with the back of her wrist, snuffled loudly and definitively, and sat up, looking at him square-on for the first time. Barr closed his ground in unconscious defense.

"Oh!" She jerked, startled. "What did you just do?"

"What did it loo—feel like I just did?" he returned cautiously.

"It's like—you were there. And then you weren't."

Barr let his ground ease open just a fraction.

"...and there you are again. Are you doing something?" She scowled in dismay.

"Yes. With some practice, Lakewalkers can close down their groundsense, turn it off for a while. As voluntary as closing your eyes. It means people can't feel into you, but it works both ways—you make yourself blind to others in turn. Which is a really welcome thing, when people make you too weary." Groundshielding's critical function in fighting malices, he suspected he'd best leave for another explanation.

She caught her breath. "When I went to Glassforge..."

"Ah, so you did go there. I couldn't figure out why you were going away from it."

"I thought it would be a place to lose myself, to maybe find work and never have to go home, but when I got there, it was all...strange. Uncomfortable. Like I was stuffed into a room with about a thousand people that would only hold twenty, and there was no air left to breathe."

Barr let his tone grow casual. "That would be normal, for a young Lakewalker dropped into such a crowd of unshielded people." The first really big farmer town he'd ever hit had thrown him totally aback, and he'd had a patroller's control by then.

"*Normal...!*" She gulped. "Normal... I thought I was going crazy." More than a hint of that breathless panic, now remembered, tightened her chest.

"If you'd grown up in a Lakewalker camp, most of the adults would keep themselves to themselves, most of the time. And you'd have had help toward working out how to shield for yourself. Plus, we don't usually live so tight together."

She shook her head in bewilderment. "I stood it for one night, sleeping in a shed, then I turned Moon around and rode out again as fast as we could. And then I didn't know where to go." Her voice squeaked painfully on this last word, but she fought back further tears.

Not back home, obviously, or she'd have turned onto the same road Barr had been traveling, and they'd have met hours ago. "I see," Barr said. Which sounded pretty vague and useless in his own ears, but maybe would encourage her to go on.

She looked up in sudden hope. "Can you teach me?"

"Not in an evening, no. It usually takes some months of practice to get a handle on it." Or years, before one was strong enough to face a malice and not get ground-ripped.

"Oh." Her face fell.

"But you could be taught in time, yes," he put in hastily. "No doubt of it."

"Oh…" She chewed on her lower lip, staring at her knees.

"Well," said Barr, which made her jump again. "It's pushing dark, and I have a tired horse to take care of." By the flicker in her, this ploy caught her attention. He clambered to his feet. "I will invite myself to share your fire tonight, but Briar comes first." Not giving her an opening to refuse his company, and cloaking his determination to stick to her in horse concerns, which seemed to work.

She watched in wary fascination as he pulled his gear from Briar's back and set about his nightly routine of horse-care, ingrained from hundreds of patrols. She'd fled Glassforge in too much of a pelter to restock rations, it appeared, because he had no trouble convincing her to share the last of his Tamarack grub, extended, and taken, with a long arm.

He prudently waited until she had some food inboard before digging out and handing across Fid's letter. He thought she'd have been happier if he'd offered her a rattlesnake, but she did take it, and, after biting her lip, ripped it open, scattering the carefully reaffixed sealing wax. She peered at the crabbed scrawl in the growing twilight, mouth moving as she sounded out the words. When she finished, she squeezed the letter into a tight ball and threw it hard onto the fire. Barr winced as it flared up, feeling for Fid.

"Good news or bad?" he asked, as if he didn't know.

She hunched, wrapping her arms around her knees and rocking. "Same stupid, stupid... Agh!" Moon, unbridled and quite unsecured, wandered over and nosed her cheek, and she leaned into him, sniffing.

Barr decided to take a chance. "They told me about the fire." He did not add, *And Edjer;* he was entailed, and there was an unfine line between prodding, and impaling through the heart.

She looked up with a bitter glare, eyes glinting blue in the firelight. "I s'ppose you think I'm a, a *ars'nist,* too."

He hardly needed the question at this point, open as she was, but she did. "Look me in the face and answer me. Did you start that fire in the barn?"

Compelled by the gravity in his voice, she did so. "No!"

"And I can see you are telling the truth."

She reared back, weirdly offended. *"Why?* Nobody else did!"

"Because I don't have to *believe.* Or guess, or judge. Groundsense is the difference between someone telling you the sky is blue, and looking up to see it with your own eyes. It's not fair to expect a blind man to make out blue." He thought he could safely leave the conclusion to her.

She mulled this for a minute, good, not flaring into argument. The wheels were turning in her head, though, for at last she said, "Can Lakewalkers even lie, then?"

"Not to each other, not easily. We can lie to farmers all right. Young patrollers can get carried away by the novelty, at first, but it turns out there are consequences." And he wasn't going to volunteer *those* stories, not tonight. No more than he would press her to tell what she hadn't added to hers, whatever bur in her hair it was. There would be time to comb that out later.

Because wherever this was going, he thought as they both settled into their bedrolls on opposite sides of the fire, it wasn't shaping up to be nearly as simple as frog-marching her back to her farm.

Blight it. He rolled over, but didn't drop off for a long time. Neither, he noted, did she.

BARR WAS GLAD he'd given himself the night to sleep on this tangle, because when he woke up, he had a plan. And it was a good one, too.

He waited till after they'd washed their faces in the creek, and tended to their horses, and Lily, wincing, had watched him scrape his knife over his face, and they'd both eaten, before he presented it to her.

"We're going to ride out this morning."

She was on her feet in an instant, fists clenched and blond braid swinging, glaring blue fire at him. "I don't want to go back to Hackberry Corner! You can't make me!"

Barr probably could, but no. "In fact, you can't go back to your farm, not the way you are now. It would be irresponsible, not to mention downright cruel." All right, hearing himself preach responsibility was like spitting cotton bolls out of his mouth, but needs must drive, as the farmers said.

It took the wind right out of her sails, anyhow. She blinked at him. "What?"

"Until you've mastered your own groundshielding, it would just thrust you back into the same painfulness you came out of. But there's a shortcut for that problem."

She sank back to her haunches. "...What is it?"

"Some Lakewalkers I know, really fine makers, developed a way a few years back to place shielding outside the body. They mostly use walnuts, but I'm told any living seed with a tight sturdy shell can anchor the shielding. And they discovered, through some trial and error, how to bind this to a farmer's ground. One of the fellows was trying to work out a way to shield his farmer wife, see."

"I...I didn't think Lakewalkers were allowed to marry farmers." She eyed him in new speculation.

"It's heavily discouraged, and he got in a lot of trouble over it—he was exiled from his camp—but more good came of that in the end than I think anyone foresaw. It sure loosened up my notions of what can and can't be done. Anyway, I can take you over to him—he and his wife's got a place at Clearcreek, about fifty miles up the Grace from Pearl Riffle. We can cut across the top of the triangle to there by riding overland on the patrol trails." Thus avoiding Pearl Riffle, Barr's tent-kin, and a host of complications, yeah. "Dag can fit you with the same kind of groundshield they're trying out on the farmer-patrollers these days. And then, well, and then you can make a choice."

"To go home? Or...what? What's the or-what?"

Barr scratched his head, grimacing. "Lily, I don't know yet. I do know I haven't worked through all the possibilities. Thing is, you don't have to do this on your own. No one else ever does, so why should you?"

Her "Oh," was very small. But thoughtful. Thing was, she would fall in behind him today without protest, which would at least get them headed the right way.

Though sometime, plainly, he needed to give her a lecture about not letting herself be talked into going off into the woods alone with strange men. But that had better wait.

Also, the ride would give Barr a chance to do some more make-up tutoring on matters Lakewalker, not that he could mend a lapse of years in a few days. Which was no excuse for not starting—doing what he could, with what he had, where he was, as Fawn would no doubt put it in her daunting downright way. There was also the chance Dag would have some idea what to do about Lily's over-beguiled horse, which even now was sniffing at her distress and trying to lick her like a foal, which at least distracted her and made her laugh, fending off slimy horse-tongue. On Barr's current list of problems, Moon wasn't even on the first page.

"Farmer-patrollers...?" she said, when she'd fallen solemn again.

"Haven't you heard about that, back at Hackberry Corner? I know Smith knows, because I've told him myself." From the smithy, the word should certainly have trickled out.

"We didn't talk about Lakewalkers at my house. But my cousin heard a rumor patrollers were picking up farmers and magicking them to be their servants."

Beating his head on a tree wouldn't be helpful, Barr supposed. "That's backwards. Shielding actually defends a person from anyone messing with their ground without leave. And it's strong—has to be, to be any use against a malice. Which *eats* ground, and sucks the life right out of you. Anything that'll defend against a malice will for-sure defend against a Lakewalker." He added conscientiously, "The farmer helpers do all the same work on a patrol that we do, side by side, except sweep for malice-sign at a distance. Or go in for a final attack." The efficiency-debates belonged to some more advanced tutorial, he reckoned.

Lily didn't even have as much gear to gather up as he did, so they were soon on their way. She rode behind him single-file into the maze of twisty patrol trails, all looking alike to the unfamiliar eye, that netted the hills southeast of Glassforge. This discouraged conversation apart from a few directions and remarks called over his shoulder. Barr had to wait to take up his thread again until their noon halt to rest the horses and themselves. They fetched up at a rocky clearing overlooking a ravine, scar of an old earth-slide.

Lily perched on a boulder; Barr stretched out his legs and put his back to another. He then amused himself by introducing her to dried plunkin, a standard and long-keeping patrol ration from his emergency supply kept in the bottom of his saddlebags.

She chewed on the leathery strip in some doubt.

"How do you like it?" Barr asked slyly.

"It's…not bad." He watched her struggle for politeness. "Better than jerky."

"I have some venison jerky, too, somewhere in there if you want." Marginally better than eating the saddlebags as it was.

"That's all right," she said, swallowing bravely. "I've never ate Lakewalker food before. Do you have this all the time?"

"Not if we can help it." Charitably, he handed across his water canteen.

"Oh." The ghost of a grin flickered over her face, which was rare and sort of enchanting. "Like parched corn cakes."

"Pretty much, yeah." He added, "The bulbs grow like a root vegetable at the bottom of lake shallows. From special-bred water lilies."

"Huh." The specter-smile faded again as she looked him over. "Can I…ask something Lakewalker?"

"You can ask pretty much anything, Lily. I'll answer as best I can." *Maybe. Depending.*

Her gaze flicked to his waist. "Is that one of those human-bone knives they talk about?"

Barr kept his voice easy. "Ayup." He drew his bonded, unprimed knife from its sheath and cradled it in his hands. Eight inches of maker-treated bone blade ran up to about four inches of wrapped hilt, just fitting his fist. The point was as sharp as bone could be polished, and his sheath was custom-built to protect it.

"Is that what patrollers stick in a blight bogle—a malice?"

"Yes. Well, not this one. It's not ready for that job yet, not primed."

"Uh, then why do you carry it around? Wouldn't a, a primed knife, whatever that is, be better?"

"Yes, and I usually have one, but I used my last primed knife on a sessile malice up in north Raintree, that I ran across coming home. Quick work, that one, which is the way I like it. I was going to beg a replacement knife at Hickory Lake Camp, where I stopped for a visit, and they would have given me one, too, but all their spares were out with patrollers that week. So I figured to wait till I hit Pearl Riffle."

"But then you went out of your way for me."

"Not very much out. Taking care of each other is as much a duty for Lakewalkers as hunting malices."

"Huh." She digested this for a spell.

All right, the next part was maybe the hardest hurdle he would have to get her over. *Don't mess this one up, Barr.* "Malices are immortal, deathless, and after they hatch will just go on eating ground, eventually killing everything around them, until the whole world is dust. I don't know if after all the malices then ate each other, the last one would starve, and I don't especially want to find out. Although I should say malices do eat, that is ground-rip, each other. Not good, because then the eater grows faster. Anyway, the reason these are called *sharing knives*"—he lifted the one in his hand—"is because they're built to share death with a malice. And the way it gets that death is from a Lakewalker. When a Lakewalker is on the verge of death—usually—the trick is to shove the unprimed, bonded knife into your own heart, so that the unmaking of your death is caught by the groundwork laid in the knife instead of going into the air, so to speak.

"This knife has been bonded to me personal by a Lakewalker knife-maker. I always keep it on me so's if I run into any fatal mishap, out and about in the world or on patrol, it's right there to stick into my heart, or get stuck into my heart, because sometimes you need help for that part. It's an act that needs physical strength at a pretty awkward angle, see. And there's no saying you'll be in condition to roll over on it, which is about the only way to get enough force to make it quick."

He glanced up to check how she was taking this, so far. She had twisted into a ball atop her boulder and was staring at him big-eyed. *Um.* He forged on.

"Patrollers all learn how to help each other to this. Now, I have no plans to fall off my horse and break my neck on this little trip, but, you know, just in case, I think we'd better have you practice a bit. So's you'd know how if you had to."

"You want me to *murder* you?"

"Sharing isn't murder."

"Help you kill yourself, then! Just as bad!"

"Sharing isn't suicide, neither. Jumping off a cliff or drowning yourself is suicide. The most shameful thing in the world to me, to most any patroller who's ever seen a malice at work, would be to *waste my death*. Way worse than...than any other dodgy thing I've ever done nor hoped not to do."

She swallowed and kept staring.

"What I've just said to you is the most important secret to ever know about us Lakewalkers. A primed knife isn't just a piece of bone, it's a mortal gift to the future, that a person can only give once. There's a whole raft of camp customs about knives, making them, bonding them, who gets to will them or keep them or carry or allot them, disposing of the broken pieces after a kill, all of it as emotional as can be, underneath. I'll try to tell you the key ones, so's if we run across another Lakewalker you won't put your foot wrong. Though I think you can guess the first rule is, don't make a big fuss about it. You just deal."

And the *next* important thing was how she had drawn in her erratic ground during his homily, ah! Just a flinch, so far, but as diagnostic as what she'd done to Moon. *We can work with this, yes.* Had watching toddler-Lily take her first steps felt something like this to Fid...? Unsettling thought. *Later.*

She lifted her chin from her tight-bent knees, where it had sunk. But the first question out of her mouth was not one he expected. *Naturally. You learning yet, Barr?* "Can those farmer-patrollers of yours...share?"

"No," he said simply. "This gets into the details of knife-making, much of which is, frankly, over my head, though you can try to get Dag or Arkady to explain it all, when we get there. They call it *affinity*. And I would purely like to know how we Lakewalkers have it with malices, and ordinary folks don't, because it has something to do with how the old mage-lords wrecked the world in the first place, and how the first malice was made and killed and burst and spread, something way over a thousand years ago. Maybe somebody will recover that history someday, but I know it won't be me. I have patrols to walk." He took a breath.

"Which brings up another thing about farmers and Lakewalkers. You know both sides discourage or outright forbid intermarriage, and you know this sometimes fails." Still more at couplings that weren't marriage, ahem. "So farmer-Lakewalker crosses are a known thing, always have been. I had to get Arkady to tell me this, once, because even I didn't learn it at home. Sometimes those crosses have enough groundsense, or maker ability, to ask to join a Lakewalker camp. The real test of whether the camp'll say *yes* is if the camp knife-maker judges the person has enough affinity to share their death. If they don't make that threshold, then they're refused."

Her face scrunched up. "So what happens if someone born in a camp doesn't have enough of this...affinity? Or does that happen?"

"Sometimes," Barr admitted.

"Are they thrown out?"

"Not usually. There's still plenty of work needs doing that doesn't take groundsense. Hence, farmer-patrollers. But they'd have trouble getting string-bound—married, you would say—and they'd be discouraged from having children."

She was of farm stock; she knew about breeding animals. She didn't seem to have trouble following this. But what she said was, "I'm beginning to see why you people keep yourselves to yourselves."

"Yeah," sighed Barr.

Her eyes narrowed to silver slits. "So...if I was to ask to join a camp, would they let me in or not? Do I have this affinity thing? Am I a Lakewalker?"

Yes, Barr did not say aloud. The inadvertent beguilement of her horse alone proved it. It was possibly the first time that imagining someone he knew choosing to share seemed a horror and not a heroism, and he was oddly shaken. And then he wondered about *his* parents, and then he wondered about all parents. He dodged the thought and the question with, "Arkady or Dag could tell, when we get to Clearcreek. For sure." Which was true enough.

And her curiosity would keep her following him all the way there, without him having to apply any cruder persuasion, good. That, and her shattered belief she'd nowhere else to go; best put off arguing her out of that.

He then jumped up and diverted her with acting out the basic techniques for assisting with a sharing, prudently using short sticks instead of the real thing or their steel knives. This seemed to go over about as well as asking her to eat worms, but she set her jaw and pushed through, right valiantly, he thought. This led, in turn, to his declaring that she needed to learn basic patroller knife-fighting styles, too, promising the first lesson at their night's halt. Upon his assurance that patroller-girls learned this, and yes, there were girl patrollers, plenty of them, including several of Barr's immediate relatives, he won her provisional assent.

And then it was time to saddle up and ride again, which seemed pretty much the story of his life.

BARR CALLED A halt at a meadow in a narrow creek valley when it was only late afternoon. There was no reason now to press their horses, after all. The next valley over, a few miles on, was flatter and farmed, and a family lived there that routinely let out their barn to passing patrols to camp in, but he wasn't just sure how comfortable Lily would be in it, what with that memory still fierce in her mind of the Mason barn burning down. Also, they'd be more likely to cross tracks with other patrollers, doubtless from Pearl Riffle and thus knowing Barr, and gabby, and he wasn't... wasn't quite ready to expose Lily to them. Explain Lily to them. Whichever. If it rained tonight, he might be sorry, but for now he wasn't.

Horse care, as always, came first, then turning their mounts loose to feed in the little meadow. Then setting up camp, as routine as breathing to Barr. Helplessly as a leaky bucket, he found himself passing on tricks and tips for efficiency in this task, just as older patrollers had taught him, and he'd taught younger patrollers in turn. Lily didn't say much—she never seemed to say much, maddeningly, weren't girls supposed to be chatterers?—but she followed

all his directions without protest. If he kept pouring information in, speaking of buckets, surely she had to fill up and
spill out something in return eventually?

In any case, he was able to use the daylight he'd saved
for a beginning lesson on knife work, directed at much
less cooperative partners than a patroller seeking to share.
How to stand and strike without just waving your knife
out for your opponent to grab off you and thus arm himself
at your expense. Then, how to move and hit someone—or
something—in motion, by far the more likely condition,
and how to see the commonest counter-blows coming and
block them. They used safety sticks again, and Barr didn't
hesitate to tap her hard to keep her awake and encourage
her to strike with some strength in return.

"I wish I had a patroller girl for you to spar against,"
he told her, when they stopped to catch breath. Barr was
not much above middle height as Lakewalkers went, though
he preferred to think of himself as *nearly tall*, but he was
built solid, so they were hardly evenly matched. "Still, if
you practice on taking out someone bigger than you are, you
should be all right for anything smaller." Which she wasn't
too likely to encounter at her current slim size, true, though
some mud-men were sawed-off little basta—buggers.

She wiped her wrist against her flushed forehead. "Is
this how you put one of those bone knives in a malice?"

"Depends. If you can find one new-hatched, still in
its larval stage, you can just about walk up to it and stick
your primed knife right in. Which is why we search hard

to find them early. If it's molted a few times and taken on form from what it's been ground-ripping—eating—it can grow a lot bigger and nastier than even its mud-men. In which case you also have to get past the mud-men to get to their maker, which can get complicated, and is why a standard patrol is a five-by-five search array, twenty-five folks. And why we train to combine patrols into a bigger company, at need."

"Have you killed a lot of those mud-men?"

"Absent gods, yes. See, every malice builds them different, plus starting out of different animals, so they come in every shape and size." He wondered if it would give her nightmares like his to tell her about the mud-bats, and decided to set that tale aside for later. It wasn't like he didn't have plenty of others. "The more advanced a malice grows, the more human-like it can make its mud-slaves. If you ever run across a mud-man that has speech, you know its malice has consumed at least one person, and we're in real trouble then."

"Huh..."

"Still, I'd twenty times rather face a mud-man, as ugly as they come, than a human bandit. Or, a hundred times worse, a person who's been mind-slaved to the malice. Because you know such folks are not, not *guilty* of anything more'n bad luck to be caught, and if only you could take down their controlling malice, they'd come back to their right minds. Every patroller hates that like poison. But sometimes it's you or them, and it had better not be you."

Her lips parted; she stared at him for a long moment. "…
Patrollers really do kill people?" *Have you?* hung unvoiced
but plain.

"*Bandits,*" he corrected, a little nettled by her tone. "River
pirates, one time. Who are not nice folks, trust me. Though
we prefer to haul them alive to the nearest farmer town and
dump them off. When we can. The local folks are usually
glad for the gift, because they're usually who the robbers
have been preying on."

It was time, he thought, to break for supper. If he filled
his mouth with food instead of words for awhile, maybe he
could stop stirring up that dark disturbance in her ground.
Fear was a plenty useful emotion, but it needed to be
directed at the right targets.

Over the campfire, once her ground had settled down a
bit, he tried his best to draw her out in turn. This was mostly
another failure, though he was able to lead her on to talk
about all the Mason horses and ponies past, and a little about
her friendship with Meggie Smith. Lily seemed to admire her.
Leading questions about her family made her clam up tight.

Eventually he gave up and started filling in the silent
gaps with some of his more benign patrol anecdotes.
Descriptions of the appalling Luthlian winters were fun for
impressing an audience, he was already finding. Though
he wasn't sure she believed him about the giant southern
swamp lizards to be found toward the delta of the great
Gray River. He had visited the Western Levels during one
of his outermost Luthlian patrols, finding them every bit as

devastated and devastating as once described to him during an evening gabfest much like this.

"What's beyond the Western Levels?" Lily asked. "How far do they go?"

"No one knows. So far, no one's been able to cross the blight without getting so drained they're either forced to turn around and go back, or they misjudge their timing and die out there in the graylands. So exploration isn't exactly encouraged."

Her silences had grown thoughtful again, not fearful, so Barr left this one undisturbed till she came out with, "Just how many patrols have you been on, anyways?"

It was Barr's turn to blink. "Lost count years ago. I started when I was sixteen, though that first year was mostly local training patrols."

"That's...only two years older'n me."

"Uh. Yeah." *Uh.* "A busy camp can field you on a patrol as often as once a month, though some sweeps in the outlying areas take longer for the getting-there. Ten a year, maybe? Let me see if I can estimate..." Arithmetic was not his strongest skill, and there had been time out for this and that, and how the blight was he to count that trip to the southern sea? It had ended up a lot more like a half-year-long patrol than a break. "More than a hundred and fifty, probably. Less'n two hundred, though."

He looked up to find her face had twisted into an expression of dismay much as when he'd first tried to explain sharing. "How old *are* you?"

"Uh…how old do I look to you?" A Lakewalker could estimate near-exactly, but then, his people judged grounds, not faces.

"Twenty…three? Maybe?"

He chuckled. "You're off by a decade. Try"—yes, a birthday had passed unnoticed during his long ride back from Luthlia—"thirty-three."

Dismay was abruptly replaced by horror. "That's nearly as old as my papa!"

Yeah, there's a reason for that, he did not force his lips to say. It was a perfect opening for a talk he did not want to have. Because if he brought her back to her farm, as he was pledged to do, he had no right to mess up her life there, now did he? Not that the Masons, among them and including Lily, hadn't managed to mess it up pretty good without his help.

He wasn't sure what his face, or his ground, looked like to her right now, but she hastily put in, "Oh! I'm sorry. I didn't mean to offend you. I wasn't trying to say you were *old* old, or anything."

"You read that reaction out of my ground, didn't you?" And never had he been more thankful that a person only sensed feelings, not thoughts.

She rocked back as if from an accusation. "Sorry!"

"No, no"—he tried to wave off her alarm gently, like a stick insect he didn't seek to damage—"I was just surprised, is all. That's a first for me. I was the youngest at home, and a youngster on patrol for so long, I'm more used to being treated like the fool than like the..." *Patrol leader?* "It was new," he finished. Lamely, he feared.

"Sorry," she repeated.

"Don't be! That was good. Shows you are starting to connect up what you feel with the meaning of it. We should practice a bit of basic ground control, while you're sensitive right now."

He then proceeded to try to show her what could hardly be told in words, opening and closing himself repeatedly. He induced some echoing twinges in her, which he made sure to praise. She seemed almost as startled by this as by her clumsy, but discernible, ground response.

A notion then crossed Barr's mind. "How do you like my mare Briar?" he asked. Briar was desultorily nibbling weeds nearby, the campfire light making her dark bay coat, now freed of its winter shagginess by Barr's labors, gleam with shifting orange highlights.

Lily followed his gaze. "She's a pretty one. She seems really fit."

"What else can you tell about her? Not with your eyes, but with your groundsense."

Lily stared for a long moment. Then offered hesitantly, "Is she...in foal?"

"Exactly right!" He made sure only satisfaction sounded in his voice, not his less comfortable emotions. "She was bred right before we left Luthlia. Should get a real fine colt out of her early next spring."

"You can tell if it's a colt or a filly?"

"Yes. Can you?"

"No..."

"Not yet, I reckon you should say," he corrected her, which induced a tremulous almost-smile.

He had possibly done something right, because when they settled into their bedrolls soon after, in the humid darkness noisy with insect and frog songs, neither of them were as strained as they'd been the night before.

Packing up their gear the next morning, Barr made the discovery that Lily had never touched a bow in her life.

"Huh!" he said. "Mine's built short to fit on my saddle and has a vicious draw, but I could still give you a beginning session or two on it. Maybe tonight." Though they'd have to ride slower than snails to fit in every lesson he kept thinking of. Knife work, bow work, ground work, how had he ever come to lodge all that in his own head? *Not in three days, for starters.* "When we get to Clearcreek, we might find something more suited to your size." Or he could get one made custom for her by some local farmer bowyer.

A bow would be a great weapon for her, he thought. It would *keep her at a distance* from mud-men. And with that innovation that Dag and Arkady were working on, making crossbow-bolt sharing knives, why, a well-shielded girl would be able to take down a malice at a nice long range. A much better picture than her closing with one of the grotesque things at armlength...

Lily didn't make any objecting noises, anyway, eying the weapon with curiosity as they mounted up. She fell in behind him on the narrow trail like a baby duckling, and conversation was curtailed again. It was a bit frightening how easy she followed him. As disturbing as how easy he took the lead?

Barr wondered when it had become such an unthinking reflex for him, when confronted with a younger Lakewalker, to start teaching his trade. Well, first there'd had to be younger Lakewalkers, he supposed. Was he, in his new anxiety, getting too much ahead of himself with Lily? Or was it just that he didn't know any way to say *I care about you* except in patroller, and when had he grown so narrow?

Or maybe the question ought to be, When had he grown enough to recognize it as narrow?

And then there were maker powers, which, he had to admit, didn't much run in Tent Foxbrush. Patrollers to the bone, his kin. Maker powers could be slower to grow than basic groundsense—Dag had been a patroller for years before he came into his own formidable crafting. Maybe Arkady could tell if Lily had any potential in that direction?

Really, he needed to stop picturing Lily as a young patroller born. She couldn't patrol anywhere unless she was fully accepted into a camp somewhere, and there were problems with it being his own. Although…really, if they were putting shielded farmers on patrols, just hitch one of those walnuts on Lily and she should be a shoo-in. Which Dag, or Arkady, or Verel, or any potent knife- or medicine-maker who'd been trained to it could fix her up with.

If she wanted. And what the blight did she want? It's not like he'd asked, in his pelter to make her safe, now had he? For all his groundsense, the girl felt as opaque to Barr as a Glassforge brick wall, even without a shield. Maybe she really wanted a farm life, if not the one she'd fled from... Maybe Fawn, adept farmwife that she was, could be a bridge to that part of Lily?

Absent gods, Barr hoped he'd find clear heads in Clearcreek, because for sure he wasn't bringing his own.

He'd been riding with his ground closed, concealing his churning mind from his attendant duckling, but a movement at the corner of his eye caught his attention. He brought Briar to a halt, turned in his saddle, and pointed, whispering, "Look!"

Lily stood in her stirrups and peered into the sun-dappled woodland. He could sense the thrill, and thrill of fear, in her when she'd seen what he had. "Bears!"

Down in the hollow they were skirting, a black bear and two cubs rooted among the fallen logs. Moon snorted uneasily as he caught the scent of them, though Briar, attuned to her rider, stayed calm. One cub reared up and tried to tackle its sibling, resulting in two furry black bodies rolling over each other and crashing into their parent, who huffed and cuffed them in a tired maternal fashion.

"Oh, they're so *cute!*" whispered Lily back. All right, so there was a thing she liked, bear cubs, although who didn't? "Can we get closer?"

"Best not try. Black bears won't usually charge a person, but Mama is going to be extra protective right now."

They stayed in their saddles for a few minutes anyway, watching the show. Or rather, Lily watched the bears, Barr watched Lily. It was fascinating how her ground lightened as she was drawn out of her sorrows for a spell, which did give Barr a clue how darkly they were weighing on her the rest of the time. Yeah, if only Edjer hadn't died, Barr thought he'd be glad to whale the tar out of the little rat for the harm his lies had done Lily. Too late to go back.

But not too late to go on. He smiled over his shoulder at Lily, who actually for the first time ever *smiled back*, huh! If briefly. Looked good on her for that moment, though. He chirped Briar into motion and led down the trail once more.

AN HOUR FARTHER on, Barr had his groundsense spread to its widest, looking for an open spot for their noon halt that would have grazing, good grass being sparse in the middle of miles of woods. The familiar, deathly bleakness just brushed the edge of the edge of his senses. He stopped Briar with a jerk, swearing aloud. The source had to be at least half a mile up the shallow creek they were fording, maybe around a bend and over a bump or two.

"What is it?" asked Lily, pulling up Moon and sounding startled at his rough words.

"There's something I need to check up this crick." Barr swung down from his saddle and dropped his reins to the path. "You stay here with the horses and *do not move*, you hear?" He thought this through. "Unless I don't come back, and then…" Yes, what? Lily could have no idea which direction to ride. He should have taught her map-reading, too, except the only one he had for this sector was in his head. "I'll be back."

He started picking his way up along the creek bed, moving as fast as he could without stumbling over the mossy rocks and breaking his leg, again. The old injury, quiet when he rode, twinged at the force he put through it hopping and striding. He breathed deep, to thwart gasping fast-and-panicked. It was fifteen endless minutes, tracking the sick sensation and steadily closing his ground as he closed the distance, before he came upon the first blight-sign, just beyond the rise out of the shallowing ravine.

He curled up tight as a walnut shell himself, dropped to the earth, and crept up over the hump to take in with his eyes what he could no longer sense with his ground. And thank the absent gods for that, or he'd be vomiting up breakfast and last night's dinner as well.

The sessile, oh, luck be praised, *still sessile* malice lay up under a bank formed by roots from a huge fallen cottonwood tree and the layered black slate of this country. This one was a pale, man-sized, vaguely man-shaped form that looked like a cross between a wet wasp nest and a grub, moist and glistening. If a grub weighed a couple of hundred pounds. If it wasn't the ugliest malice Barr had ever seen, or the most terrifying, that maybe said more about Barr than about the gestating monster. But it couldn't move on its own, yet.

Its next molt, changing out like a caterpillar splitting its carapace for the new form now growing inside it, would fix that, though, Barr judged. The bloated skin rippled as the new one turned and jerked inside its parent.

If only he'd possessed a primed knife, he could walk up and finish it right now. *Yeah. Crap.*

The woods for a hundred paces around were dead and gray, weeds dried brittle, trees leafless, worse than a patch of winter dropped down into spring's lap. A couple of desiccated rabbit and squirrel corpses lay around the margins; farther in, any little critter that had mischanced to cross the blight was already rendered down to a pile of formless ash.

Barr dared to rise and creep closer, peering hard for the pots, the holes in the soil where the new malice, immobile as it still was, might already be brewing up its first batch of mudmen slaves. Who would not be immobile at all, and whose first task would be to range out and collect more living creatures to feed their master. If his luck held, it was still too soon...

Nope. Double crap. Some five or six barrel-wide bumps lay in the earth around the lair like the tops of oversized, misshapen combs in a wasp nest, nursery for larvae. The pots' swollen surfaces betrayed their quasi-living contents, passing animals captured and subjected to this malice's budding groundwork, forms changing from the inside out.

The *Why the blight didn't the Pearl Riffle patrol find this thing before now?* question was answered by the malice's newness. The patrol was lucky if it could cover every outlying sweep in its region once a year. Closer in, like here, might get checked every six months, but this malice couldn't be older than three months.

Three months from now it was going to be a lot easier to find, hah. It might even be on the march to find people itself, whatever unprotected farms lay with ten or twenty miles; or worse, stray Lakewalkers. Worse for everybody, including the Lakewalkers, because then the malice would be abruptly boosted to many times its present mage-skills.

Or maybe three days from now—its gravid engorgement promised the next molt very soon.

Well, let's not feed it a stray Lakewalker today, eh? Barr began to back out.

And into a soft body.

He whipped his hunting knife out and whirled around so fast he nearly sliced Lily, who'd come up behind him unsensed by his closed ground and unheard, well, he'd no idea what was wrong with his ears, apart from the wildest distraction. *"I told you to stay put!"* He'd meant it for a fierce whisper, but it came out more of a strangled shriek.

She recoiled, the hand that had touched his shoulder hiding behind her, but then her gaze and her groundsense swung to the malice huddled under the slate bank. Her eyes sprang wide and her face drained green. *"What is that?"*

"That's a sessile malice, and *it can sense you.*" The long lump was already reacting, bucking in helpless excitement. "You didn't bring the horses up, did you?" A pregnant mare, gods, that thing would love a pregnant mare. After ground-ripping Briar, it would probably molt on the spot.

It would relish Lily much more, however.

"Tied Moon to a tree by the path. He was trying to follow me. I don't know if Briar stayed with him." Her face bunched in distress. "You didn't come back. I got scared!"

Barr knew a raft of rivermen's invective, inventive and blistering, and it all eluded him in his present need. "Crap. Crap. *Crap.*" He drew breath. "Now we run. Back to the path."

But Lily was looking past him. "What is *that*, now?"

Barr spun on his heel in time to see a not-quite-finished mud-man erupt out of its pot in the damp soil like a boil bursting. Raccoon core, probably, although it was grown to man-sized. It lurched toward them, black slime spinning off patchy wet fur and blood-red skin.

"Retreat." He grabbed her arm and dragged her with him, moving backward over the rise. With every stride, the raccoon-man was finding its balance, picking up its pace. The distorted creature was moving too blighted fast. Barr couldn't make out, in the blur, if its black claws tipping too-human hands had hardened to killing sharpness, or were still soft. But it looked like he was going to find out real soon. "Run and don't stop, back to the horses!"

That would put Lily temporarily out of range, if this malice was advanced enough to try for mind-slaving instead of just consumption. It didn't seem as if more than the one mud-man had been ripe enough to be deployed. Barr put himself between it and Lily, raising his knife. He slashed it good, incoming, but it barreled right into him anyway. They both went tail over teakettle, rolling down the slope toward the trickle of creek, bouncing painfully off saplings and slamming over tree roots that hit like cudgels.

A muddy knee-like joint landed on his knife-arm, and two big hands closed around his neck. *Gods* the thing stank at this range. Though if it had its way, in a moment he wouldn't be breathing, solving that problem naturally. He squeezed his own knee up between them, heaving the thing off him and breaking its hold at the price of half-mangling his neck. He scrambled to his feet.

It came up after him swinging—maybe it had been a *wolverine*—and Barr dodged harrowing claws, trying for a slash any-which-way under its guard. His boot slipped in the damp leaf litter on the slope, twisting his bad leg, and he howled obscenities that he shouldn't ought to be saying in front of Lily, where was *Lily*—

A loud, wet *plonk* echoed, like somebody'd thrown down a muskmelon from a second-story window onto a cobbled street. The mud-man staggered forward from the bash on the back of its head delivered by a log like half a fence rail, swung with all her might by Lily. She swung again and again, blond braid bouncing, screeching like a farmwife frightened by a mouse: "Eeek! Eew! Ugh! *Eew, eew!*"

Absent gods, any mouse crossed *her* kitchen floor was going to be *paste*.

The mud-man, which in addition to not living quite right, didn't die quite right, kept heaving around at her feet as she bashed away, so she didn't stop either. "*Die,* you ugly thing!"

Leg throbbing, Barr found his balance, such as it was, and watched open-mouthed. Knife work, bow work, ground work...yeah, her method worked, too.

Oh, my aching head, she's so cute! So cuuute...! It wasn't till the bludgeoned beast stopped heaving and took to feeble twitching that he was able to break out of his arrested enchantment.

Also because Lily dropped her log, backed up, clutched her belly, bent over, and started violently hurling up her breakfast.

Aye, her first blight burn. Let's get the crap away from here. Ow, Ow... He limped down to her, grabbed her arm, and said, "You can keep barfing, but start walking. This way."

"You're bleeding!" she cried between halts for heaves. He wasn't sure if her tears were for the terror or the nausea, both justified, but in either case he did the polite thing and passed no comment on them. "I thought you were killed!"

"Not dead while I can still swear." Barr dabbed at his neck. His fingers came away wet and red. "Ayup. Scratches aren't deep, though." *Or they'd have taken out an artery. Let's not think about that.* "We'll need to clean them soon as we get back to the horses and before we ride, though, because those claws were *filthy*."

"Ride where?" she gulped.

"Yeah, I'd better decide quick, shouldn't I." The three closest camps to their present location were Log Hollow, Muskrat Slough, and Pearl Riffle, and Pearl Riffle was less than half the distance of the other two. They could ride to it in one long, brutal day. It wasn't even a choice.

Unless they threw lucky and ran across a patrol on the way, Barr supposed. Yeah, best not count those unhatched chickens.

We're both alive. You can't ask for more luck in one day than that.

"And the next lesson," he wheezed as they splashed down the creek bed, "is that when your patrol leader tells you to stay put, you blighted *stay put.*"

She didn't seem nearly impressed enough by his muted fury, maybe because he was having trouble with the *fury* part. *Cute* was remarkably disarming, as was being wracked with relief.

"I was afraid—if you'd had one of those primed knives, you'd have stuck it right into that horrible thing, right?"

"Oh, yes. And this emergency would be over. I wish."

"I was terrified you'd make me help you prime *your* knife, and then I'd have to stick it in the malice myself." He wasn't sure which half of that appalled her more. With his ground closed, he had to judge her mood by her face. She looked pretty distraught. Her stomach spasms were passing off, though; she bent and scooped up a handful of water from the creek, rinsed her mouth, and spat. And stood resolutely up and wobbled on, though she watched him sideways.

"I...won't say such an act has never played out before in patrol history, but it wouldn't have worked today in any case. If you'd got any closer to that malice, unshielded as you are, it would've ripped your ground right out of you, and you'd've been dead before you could strike." Barr shuddered, disguised in his general stumbling. "No, we just follow standard procedures for a case like this. Later, we need to talk about the *following orders* parts of those. But first we ride like madmen for the nearest camp and report the malice sighting. And they send out a patrol to take care of it properly equipped."

"Oh…" Her blond brows crimped. "Will I get to see a real Lakewalker camp, then?"

"Yeah," Barr sighed, concealing his anticipatory cringe. "Pearl Riffle's closest."

"Wait, isn't that your home?"

"Ayup. The blight burn in your ground is going to make you sick for a few days, but sick or no, you're going to have to keep up with me. Moon will follow Briar"—he would make sure of it—"so you just need to stick in your saddle. When we get there, Maker Verel will be able to help the worst of it, so keep thinking on that."

What else would await her when they arrived, Barr couldn't even begin to guess.

Blight. Blight. Blight…

THEY DROPPED DOWN from the patrol trails into the great valley of the Grace River as full darkness overtook them. Barr thought he could navigate at this stage with his ground closed and a sack over his head just by the familiar smells. The sweep of the stars above and their answering glint on the wide, moving waters lifted his heart despite all his distractions. He'd missed this place more than he'd known, seemed like.

The last five miles or so on the well-maintained farmer road were the easiest going they'd had all day, thankfully, because Lily'd folded into a silent bundle of misery clinging to her saddle, too sick to complain. It was unfortunate that the most efficient pace for the grueling trek was a trot that was hard on a nauseated rider, though they'd been forced to a walk over the more rugged stretches. Briar was holding up, but Moon was flagging. Barr'd saved what time he could by limiting breaks to watering stops. Food was out of the question for Lily, but after all that barfing he needed to keep her from becoming dangerously parched.

When they angled off the river road up toward the northeast gate of his home camp, Barr's throat tightened, ambushed by stupid tears. *Tired, that's all it is.* And those stupid clawings, that kept opening up and leaking under the makeshift bandage wrapped around his neck. And the stupid bruises, that sapped strength even when their pain was ignorable. He gulped down all his stupid and led on.

The entry was guarded as usual by a couple of patrollers on camp rest, sitting on stumps under the light of a bright rock-oil lantern up on a pole. They were occupying their hands and time by spinning twine, but they set down their task and rose as the two horses emerged out of the darkness.

"Who goes—oh! Young Barr Foxbrush, as I live and breathe! So you didn't freeze up in Luthlia after all!"

Emie Heron; he'd patrolled with her any number of times. With the fellow, too, though he didn't recall his name right off.

"More like to be sucked to death by the ticks, but yeah, I'm back. Can't stop. We came across a sessile malice way up in Sector Six, and I'd no primed knife with me. I need to report it to Captain Amma."

"Right. Go." She gave way instantly, although her brows rose as he passed into the circle of light. "Looks like it came across you, too!"

"Medicine tent'll be the next stop. Verel home?"

"Should be." He barely caught her trailing mutter as the two riders passed by, "Now who's that he's got with him…?"

Comfortable lights speckled the hillside, families settling down into their tents—which farmers insisted were actually cabins—for the night. Barr picked out and then studiously ignored the kin cluster that was Tent Foxbrush, barely visible through trees full with new leaf. A whiff from the tannery, down by the waterside, wrinkled his nostrils. A warmer whiff of horses from the patrol paddocks chased it as they skirted around, and both their mounts snuffled and twitched curious ears.

At length, Barr turned in and pulled up before the foursquare clapboard building that was the patrol headquarters. A yellow glow from oil lamps shone through the glass windows—good, folks were still about. He opened his ground enough to announce himself to those within, and the reverse—ah, there was Amma in person; they wouldn't have to hunt up the camp patrol captain from her dinner.

"Are we there yet?" moaned Lily into Moon's mane as she was at last allowed to halt. The gelding's head drooped.

"Ayup. You just stick tight up there for a little longer. I shouldn't be more'n five minutes inside, and then we can get you to the medicine tent."

"You've been saying that fer *hours*. Lyin'…liar."

That was unfortunately so. With a guilty pang, Barr left her to her wilt and hobbled within.

Amma Osprey was already rising to her feet from her lamplit writing table as he closed the door behind him. "Barr! You made it back! Your tent-kin have been looking out for you for the past month."

A rare smile lightened her angular features—very rare, to have directed at him. He sopped it up while he could get it. She was still tall, lean, wearing everyday patrol garb of boots, trousers, shirt with the sleeves rolled up, and long leather vest. Her hair was barely grayer, although he flinched a bit to see it bound again in a tight mourning knot at her nape. Tent Osprey was far-flung; it need not be for someone too intimate, though he wondered if there was a new primed knife in the camp arsenal. If she didn't volunteer the details, he wouldn't make remark, at least not now.

As she took in his bedraggled state her mouth screwed up, consuming the smile. "Right, boy, what tried to take your head off? This time."

"Mud-man. Lots to tell"—*and not tell*—"but first thing, we ran across a sessile at the top of Sector Six. I didn't have a primed knife on me, so we scarpered straight for camp."

"Why didn't you have a knife? Didn't those stingy Luthlians send you home with one?"

"They did, but I used it on a sessile I ran across in north Raintree. Sent the pieces and the thank-you letter back by the courier from Hickory Lake."

"Ah. Good on you, then. And on them." She charitably didn't ask if the knife's death had been someone he knew.

Turning to open the map cabinet, she pulled out the relevant chart, which she flung across the big table in the center of the room like a sheet settling over a bed. Bony hands spread, smoothing it out. "That area was last combed-through just four months back. Training patrol. Did they miss a section?"

"Maybe not. I didn't judge this sessile had been growing for much more'n three months, though it looked to be right on the verge of its first molt. It did have its first batch of mud-men brewing." He laid his thumb down on the spot he gauged nearest the sighting, and Amma nodded.

"When?"

"Around noon today."

"You made good time." She frowned at the map. "But what were you doing way up there?"

"Shortcut to Clearcreek."

"What, off to see that Dag fellow before you even checked in with your own kin? Or me?" She gave him a side-eye. He shrugged, which seemed safer than saying anything.

She strode for the door to the back room and shouted through it, "Ryla! Drop what you're doing and go tell Fin to get his reserve patrol ready to ride out at dawn. Supplies for four days." She glanced over her shoulder at Barr. "Or more?"

"Not much more. It only had six mud-men ready to pop, and we took out one of them."

"Make that five days," she amended her direction. "And stop on the way at the medicine tent, tell Verel he's got an old customer coming."

"Two customers," Barr put in.

She turned her head toward the front of the building beyond which Lily wearily waited. "Ah, I see…" She leaned back into the doorway and corrected, "Couple of 'em. A youngling with her tail dragging, and Barr Foxbrush back from Luthlia with his usual shenanigans."

"Yes, ma'am!" came the return call, followed by the sound of quick bootsteps and the rear door slamming.

Amma turned back to Barr. He could just about watch the calculations of people, equipment, horses, time and distance rolling over in her captainly head. But she said, "Who's your partner? You bring an exchange patroller back from Luthlia?" A puzzled frown as her groundsense flicked out again. "No…too young to be an exchange patroller. Too young to be any patroller!"

"You wouldn't say that if you could have seen her take down her first mud-man today," said Barr, torn between pride and wariness.

"How'd you come to be trailing a youngster? You pick her up from another camp? Courierin' her somewhere?"

"Long story," he evaded this. "Tell you tomorrow." *Unless I can duck you.* "Right now I need to get her over to the medicine tent. Because she also took her first blight burn, and then I made her ride after me all day. She's sick as a pup."

"No argument here. Your day's done, get along with you." Her brow furrowed as she studied him, gaze lingering on the soaked bandage. "That one looks like a little too close a shave. I thought you were over turning up looking like something the catamount dragged in, or I wouldn't have sent you off to plague poor Luthlia."

"Yeah, yeah. Sweet on you too, Amma." He made a gesture in the general vicinity of a salute, and retreated while he still had his hide intact. Apart from his neck.

"Good job, Barr!" she called after him. "And your young friend! Welcome home!"

Uncommon praise from Pearl Riffle's stern camp captain. He smiled bleakly and slipped out the door like a fish, closing it behind him before she could glimpse Lily.

The climb back up onto Briar seeming insurmountable, he took the reins of both horses and limped off into the cozy darkness. "Not far to go."

"Doan b'lieve you."

"Now, now." This close to help, Barr was finally able to be amused.

After a shortish walk angling up the slope, the clapboard structure that was Pearl Riffle's medicine tent loomed out of the shadows. It was of a similar vintage to the patrol headquarters, built when the older log cabins, settling into decay, had been replaced with new water-mill-sawn farmer lumber from nearby Pearl Bend. The building had acquired yet another add-on while Barr had been gone, he noted. A tallow-candle lantern, hung on a hook above the door, offered a dim guidelight. Brighter lamps were being lit inside, so apparently Verel had received the word of their coming.

Lily raised her head and stared blearily. "Tha's notta tent. Looks just like a house to me."

"Lakewalker talk, when we're being polite about our lapses. I'll explain later." He dropped both horses' reins and went to her stirrup. "Come on down, now." She did not so much dismount as slump off into his arms. He steered her up the steps.

She turned her head. "Horses. Moon."

"They'll be taken very good care of shortly. For once, patrollers first."

"Oh."

He pushed open the door to find three people in the front room, a man, a woman, and a boy, who all looked back with acute interest.

Verel Owlet hadn't changed much in two years, Barr was relieved to see: still lean, clean, and fiftyish, hair in a neat black braid down his back. His coppery skin betrayed northern ancestry—Barr's paler Foxbrush coloration had likely come upriver from the south a few generations back. Barr blinked to recognize the tallish, black-haired boy at the chief maker's elbow as one of his sons, Quen.

Verel grinned at his entry. "Well, if it isn't a familiar face. Good to see you back, Barr!" The medicine maker's extremely keen groundsense licked out, making a quick first evaluation of the healing tasks that had just landed on his doorstep. "And an unfamiliar face, too… Good grief, Barr, where in the wide green world did you find yourself a daughter?"

Barr made a frantic throat-cutting motion which, given his gory bandages, did not seem to be immediately understood.

Lily mumbled into his shoulder, on which she was leaning, "We're not related. Just have the same hair color, 's all."

Barr overrode Verel's, "You most certainly are!" with a louder, "This here's Miss Lily Mason from Hackberry Corner, out at t' west end of Sector Nine, and she's had a blight burn and a long, bad day. Hope you can help with both."

"Of course," said Verel, giving him a perplexed look, followed by a more kindly maker's smile to Lily. He added, "I should introduce my new apprentice, Yina Mink. She came on soon after you left for Luthlia, I believe, transferred down from Log Hollow medicine tent to study with me."

The woman ducked her head cheerfully at Barr and Lily. She seemed younger than Barr, though not a youngling, with coloration betwixt and between, her reddish-brown hair tied out of the way in a queue at her nape. A simple ankle-length skirt and shirt with the sleeves rolled up, topped by a well-washed, if stained, linen apron, suggested someone who'd come prepared for messy labors.

"She's actually just back from a two-month rotation with Dag and Arkady at Clearcreek," Verel went on, "so you two may have tales to share, later. She's interested in their farmer schemes."

Barr was diverted by that last bit, but, "Later," he said firmly. "Uh..." His wits, normally quick to self-preservation, were slowing with fatigue, but did manage this much: "Once you're done torturin' me, can Lily and me bunk in here tonight?"

"You know we don't house the walking wounded, don't you want to get home..." He trailed off, eyeing Barr. And Lily. Verel was not slow-witted at any time. "But it's not as if we don't have the bunks, the latest patrols not being home yet," he continued smoothly. "Yina, please take Miss Mason here and get her a light ground reinforcement, a drink, a bath, and a clean nightshirt. Check for any other damage. I'll cope with the smelly patroller."

At Lily's plaintive look and jerky gesture, Barr put in, "Quen—that is Quen, isn't it? Absent gods, you're taller. Can you please pull our saddlebags down and take our horses over to the patrol paddocks? Let the girls on duty know they've put in a hard day's work."

At a nod from his father, Quen grinned and trotted out. Lily, warily, allowed herself to be drawn off by Yina. "It'll be all right!" Barr called after her. "Just do what she tells you."

Verel took up an oil lamp and gestured Barr into the front treatment room, sitting him on a stool. There followed a contemplative silence while he laid out the tools of his trade, then went off to collect a basin of clean water. Some soaking, scissors, and a touch of groundwork detached Barr's bandage from the crusts and red ooze underneath. Verel grimaced. "Those are interestingly ugly."

Interesting was never a good word to hear from a medicine maker. "Mud-man clawings. Might have been uglier, if the claws had grown harder."

"I see that. Touch of blight burn here, too." Barr could feel Verel's soothing ground reinforcement go in. Then less-soothing cleaning around the wounds with spirit-soaked cotton wads, more firm and thorough than gentle, which made him hiss. "So what about that girl, Barr? And don't try to tell me she's not your daughter."

"Half farmer," Barr got out through gritted teeth, and not just for the horsing around on his neck.

"Really? ...Barr!"

"It was almost fifteen years ago! I was another man then. Boy, I suppose."

"I remember."

"Everyone here does," Barr sighed. "I hoped my stint in Luthlia might cure that." He watched in disfavor as Verel turned to thread up a curved needle. "Can't you use ground-work for that?"

"I'm not the Clearcreek crew, thank you. And even they'd stitch these. Stretchy skin."

"*Ow,*" whimpered Barr as Verel began to demonstrate. "I was young and dumb. I thought I could get away with something. Didn't find out how wrong I was till two, almost three years later. After that trip to the sea. Ow."

"Go on."

"In maker's confidence?"

Verel pursed his lips. "Maker's judgment is all I can promise. And due care for the girl."

Due care could have all too many possible meanings. Barr didn't trust Verel quite as much as he trusted Dag, but the maker was likely to be more objective than anyone in Tent Foxbrush. And bringing the lading of these heavy secrets to some safe harbor was suddenly, horribly seductive. *Ow.*

"It's a long story."

"That's fine. This is going to take a few minutes." As long as needed to get the tale all cleaned out of him, like an old infection? Verel was relentless by trade, as the next needle poke reminded Barr.

Reluctantly, then less so as his account reached the more recent events, Barr made his confession, punctuated by pained yips. Verel didn't much interrupt, except with the meticulous work of his hands. They both finished about together, which Barr didn't take for a coincidence. His hand went to his neck, and was firmly brushed away.

"Dirty paws off, till you wash up."

"Did it really need that blighted many stitches?"

"I was sewing up ribbons in places, here. Try for some gratitude."

"Yessir."

Verel sighed. "Your young Lily's had a dreadful time of it the past month or so, sounds like."

"So I make it." Although Barr still smiled every time he thought of that flattened mud-man.

"What were you planning to do about it all?"

"Take her to Dag and Fawn in Clearcreek. I thought I could get good advice from both sides, farmer and Lakewalker, there. And get her one of those walnut ground-shields made custom. If she wanted to go home. Or on, for that matter."

"That...actually wasn't a bad scheme." Verel's praise would feel more flattering if he didn't sound quite so surprised.

"It still could be. I was thinking we might slip out of camp early tomorrow morning."

"That girl is not going to be ready for a fifty-mile ride tomorrow. And neither are you."

"Hey, we just did forty!"

"And your horses?"

"Mm..."

"Uh-huh." Verel's dry growl spoke of decades of arguing with mule-headed patrollers, and winning.

Barr stared down at his hands, every bit as grubby as Verel claimed. "...Could she share?" he blurted.

"Hm?"

"In your judgment. As a medicine maker. Could Lily join a camp?" *Could she join this one?*

Verel sucked his lower lip. "I'd have to take a closer look at her, but my first impression was certainly Lakewalker."

So had Amma's been, Barr was reminded. And that Muskrat Slough courier's.

"It will be at least another year before her powers settle in past that first rocky rush," Verel continued. "As you likely remember as well as I do. And some growing at a slower pace after. But given the start she's made in, what, you said six months, yes. Now, *which* camp is another question. Some being more rigid than others."

"I know," said Barr. Any camp in Luthlia would take Lily in a heartbeat, Barr suspected; that pressed hinterland was notorious for accepting anyone who could ride, sense, and brought a primed knife or even just a bonded one, no questions asked. He'd been invited to stay himself. But Luthlia was a thousand miles off, up around the west end of the Dead Lake. Camps to the south were pickier about farmers and farmer blood; granted, camps to the north didn't have farmer neighbors. *Yet.* As Dag was fond of grimly pointing out.

So, it was not a camp, maybe not even this camp, that was the hurdle. Which left Tent Foxbrush. Very proud patrollers, Tent Foxbrush. As rattle-pated boys who did not live up to their family's expectations had pointed out to them, repeatedly. *I really do not want to deal with this.*

Barr sighed. "Does that bath and nightshirt offer go for me, too?"

Verel smirked. "Especially the bath. Patroller reek, whiffy!"

"Your favorite perfume, Verel."

"Heh. Just our most familiar." But Verel lifted a lamp as Barr creakily unbent from the stool, the maker's other hand going out to stop a stumble. Barr winced and shrugged it off, limping after the light through the medicine tent and out the side door.

On the short, covered boardwalk to the pump-and-bathhouse, Barr heard Lily's voice, raised and distraught.

"That can't be right. He kept trying to teach me all these horrible patroller things, and I don't want to know any more! I never seen a blight bogle before and I hope I never see one again! I *can't* be a Lakewalker—" She broke off abruptly as Verel and Barr made their way into the flagstone-paved chamber; its tricky Tripoint iron pump had replaced the old open well out in the yard only a few years back.

Lily was perched on a stool, rocking anxiously. Judging from her hair, darkened tawny from the damp and hanging in washed tangles down her back, the bath had been accomplished. Her nightshirt was oversized and threadbare, though boiled clean, typical of the outworn clothing folks donated to the medicine tent to take its last abuse from leaky patients. Yina's treatment must have cut in—Lily's yelping was a good sign, really; if the blight nausea were lingering she would still be too limp and green to be upset. *What* she was saying, though...

"How's she doing?" Verel asked his apprentice. Senior apprentice, Barr guessed, from her impressive maker's ground density.

She turned to him in open relief. "Ground reinforcement onboard, drank all she'll hold, splinters out of her hands, ointment and bandages to the saddle sores on her knees, which hadn't rubbed too deep. They'll scab and heal up on their own if she stays off a horse for a few days. All that's left is hunger and exhaustion, and I think she's about ready to try a bite." Yina smiled at Lily in tentative encouragement.

"And a bed is waiting to take care of the other, eh?" She added to Verel, "No other injuries. All in all, a healthy and intact young woman."

"That's good to hear."

Barr thought so, too, and then the double meaning of that polite 'intact' cut in. *Oh.* He was suddenly glad not to be a medicine maker, although patrol leaders, too, had to deal with every kind of human hurt, on the fly and with fewer supplies. Still, it was like noticing a dangerous drop only after you'd drawn back from it, a spot of retroactive dizziness.

Lily swung around and up onto her bare feet, scowling fiercely at Barr. "Tell them it isn't so!"

"Which isn't so?" said Barr, confused again. Or this might be his new permanent state.

Her hand circled and fell back, as if trying to encompass everything and failing. "That patroller fellow is not my papa!" she insisted to the makers.

Yina said placatingly, "Well, that ground congruence might be uncle or brother, but it sure looks like father to me."

"No, not any! Tell, them, Barr! My papa is Fid Mason of Hackberry Corner!"

Ah. Barr cleared his throat, feeling sheepish and small. There was no more putting this off, plainly. "In every important way but one I think he really is, Lily." With an effort, he kept himself from closing his eyes tight as he spoke, like a youngster getting a stitch put in. "But...yeah. Not quite fifteen years ago, I was a young patroller visiting Hackberry

Corner. My patrol camped for a few days on your grandparents' farm. Where I met your mother. We, er, fancied each other. Things happened."

"That's not possible. Mama *hates* Lakewalkers!"

"Well," Barr sighed, "she didn't then. I rode off, things happened to me... You were rising two by the time I ever got back around there. Surprise to me. Your mama told me to back the blight off—well, she didn't say *blight*—and stay away, so I did.

"But I kept an eye on you, time to time, till I transferred up two years ago to the hinterland of Luthlia. On the way home last week I found your place burned down, deserted, which gave me quite a turn. So I rode around till I found your family at your aunt's, but you weren't there. And the rest you know."

"No," Lily whispered miserably. "I don't *want* to be a Lakewalker anymore..." Her voice rose in a new outrage. "And you, you *knew* all along, and you didn't *say...?*" The outrage edged into horror. "I was startin' to get *sweet* on you!"

"Huh?" said Barr.

Verel leaned over, took aim, and flicked him hard with a fingernail upside his head. "And there's *another* good reason for being more honest, sooner, Barr!"

Barr and Lily glowered at each other with equal, he thought, if differently angled, dismay. Yes, he'd wanted her to like him, sure, if only to make keeping her on the right trail easier, but not that way! He choked out, "I didn't think you'd care for the news."

"Well, you're right!" She crossed her arms tightly, chin thrust out. Trembling. "Explains why you're so *old*, though!"

Was that supposed to be some kind of counter-stab? And how had they descended to stabbing each other, anyway?

"Look, Lily. No one, not even me, could know you were going to throw to your Lakewalker side until you did, this past half-year. Throw strong, even less. And if you didn't, if you hadn't, it seemed best to leave things as they lay, over there in Hackberry Corner. Like your mother wanted. But it didn't work out that way, so you're my responsibility now, will or nil."

"Nobody asked you to take responsibility for me!" she snapped, then hesitated. "…Did they? Anyhow, I know *I* didn't!"

Helplessly, he scratched his grimy head. "It doesn't work that way. Patrol rules. If you're the one who can, the one in position, you're the one who does. You don't *wait*." Well, there'd been his imagined reinforcements at Clearcreek, toward which he'd been retreating with all the speed he could muster, but waving Dag and Fawn at her seemed pretty pointless when she still didn't even know who they were. What they were. …What she was.

"So, am I one of your blight bogles now? As well as a farmer? Pick one! Just so's you don't pick Lakewalker!"

"No—look—that's, that, who you are, it's not something you can *choose*. Nor me neither. It just *is*!"

Verel and Yina exchanged an unreadable look.

"I'm sorry," said Yina hesitantly. "It seems I shouldn't have spoken."

Barr waved this off. "Not your fault. Nobody told you." There'd been no private moment to warn her away from his secrets, nor had he marshaled the wits to make one.

"But—" Her head tilted. "My word, Verel, how many stitches did you put in him? He looks like a quilt."

"Forty-three," said Verel, with a certain makerly satisfaction. He swung the lamp to cast light on his work.

Lily fell still, staring at Barr's neck. In a much smaller voice, she said, "You claimed they were just scratches."

"So they were," said Barr. "Didn't tear through any muscles much, didn't rip a big blood vessel. Or I wouldn't be here to complain."

Verel snorted. "Patrollers. Bane of my life." He set the lamp down. "Later, we will discuss the wonders of adhesions, but for now, Yina, please clear the washroom for us, and get what food you can into that tired young lady, eh? And get her tucked in."

Separating the combatants? Might be wise.

Lily's tight face looked as if she was stuck between anger and tears, and Barr wasn't sure which he'd rather, or rather not. The sight was surprisingly painful. But Yina nodded understanding, of the direction and likely the undercurrent as well, and shepherded her charge out. Lily looked back in worry at Barr as his fingers began to fumble at his shirt, all streaked brown and dried stiff. Briefly, Yina followed her gaze.

As the door swung closed, he called after them, "You did terrific well at the malice sighting, Lily!" He couldn't see how she took it.

Verel watched him pick for another moment or two, then sighed, shifted over, and began undoing the obstinate buttons himself. It made Barr feel about five years old. He could almost wish he still was.

"This...wasn't how I'd planned to tell her. About me 'n her."

"Uh-huh."

"I mean, I suspected it wasn't going to go down well, but I thought I'd best try to get Lily to understand what it meant to be a Lakewalker, first."

"Sounds like she's had a pretty intense tutorial for only three days." Verel peeled the shirt off him and set it aside to await a soak. "You know, I've never witnessed a malice, not even a sessile, in my whole life."

"Well, sure." Barr shrugged. "With your groundwork talents, they'd have nailed you down for a maker before you were out of your teens, I expect. Kept you safe in camp." Insofar as camps were safe, and that was Barr's job, wasn't it? "They taught you basic patrolling before then, though, right? Every youngster gets that."

"Oh, yes. Point is..."

But Barr didn't find out what the point was, because Quen came bouncing in, and Verel promptly drafted him to work the pump handle. There followed contortions to get the patroller wet but keep the stitches dry, strong soap, and a bonus debate on whether Barr's bruises, purpling impressively, counted as injuries or not. Quen was assigned the picking-up-after, and Verel led Barr, in a nightshirt that could have stood to be a mite bigger, off to the promised bunk in the men's chamber.

Barr wanted to keep arguing, but the sight of that clean, soft bed in the yellow lamplight was almost enough to make him burst into tears. He took possession before he could disgrace himself. Further.

IN THE DEEP night, Barr lurched awake to a loud and heartbroken whinny seeming to come from right outside his window. A staccato thumping of shod hooves trailed away, circling the medicine tent. This was followed by another whinny, even longer and more reverberant, and a knocking from the other side of the building like someone trying to bash in the wall with a sledgehammer. Lily's startled, muffled voice sounded from somewhere over in the women's bunkroom. The knocking stopped, but then began again from the side stoop.

Barr rolled his sleep-stiffened body out of bed, cursing as his bad leg twinged something fierce. He limped through the shadows to the side door. Lily's pale form dodged ahead of him. Had she developed dark vision yet? Which wasn't so much vision, as ground awareness of the hazards before you tripped over them, *Ow, blight it!* The door banged open as Lily ran through, which at least stopped the ruckus before Verel's door was kicked in, plus whatever damage a panicked horse barging around inside might do.

Barr rubbed his shin and pushed through the door that had slammed in his face, taking in the scene. Which had all the overwrought emotion of a reunion after six years, not six hours, ugh. *Not enough sleep.* In the light of the westering moon, the gelding lived up to his name, looking an astral sort of being. Lily in her fluttering nightshirt matched him for ethereal glow. Barr cringed for her bare toes so near those dancing hooves, but the horse quieted right down as she hugged him around the neck and crooned, "Oh, clever, clever Moon! You came to find me, didn't you? Were you afraid, all alone?"

Barr thought him a fool beguiled beast with the brains of a rabbit, but this did not seem the time to say so. Lily embraced him as if he were her only friend in all the world, which…was sadly true right now, wasn't it? The only piece of her home she still possessed. Because she'd abandoned whatever human friends she'd had along with her family, leaving all bonds equally broken in her wake. Save this one. *Were you afraid, all alone…?*

Barr sighed deeply and leaned against a porch post flanking the steps, waiting till the two had calmed each other down.

"Or trying to rescue me? Dear Moon! But it's no good to have a horse to ride and nowhere to *go*." She rubbed his flopping ears, and he leaned into her hand. "Not even you can fix that."

"He didn't exactly come to you on his own, you know," Barr observed from his prop. "You called him. Maybe not quite on purpose. Some patrollers do that, with their mounts. I can. If you aren't set to grow powers at least equal to the average patroller, Lily, I'll eat my saddle."

Releasing a last pent breath, she turned his way, leaning against Moon's shoulder and folding her arms in an unwitting echo of Barr's pose. Or maybe she was just as exhausted as he was. "Are you an average patroller?"

Barr cleared his throat. "Maybe a mite better." He contemplated those words for a moment. "No—stronger. Stronger's just born. Better's learned. Which is a long road with a lot of hard knocks. I suppose it's a bit crazy to want you to learn in a week what took me decades."

Is it? She was a smart child, or she couldn't have got herself this far, beguiled horse be hanged. All tense lips and straight spine, cloaking a bristling bundle of terror, hurt, month-old outrage, betrayal, and loneliness—it would be safer to try to pet an injured porcupine.

"Lakewalkers aren't built to be alone," Barr went on. "Because these are real powers, mage powers, although no one calls them that, the old mages having given themselves a bad name. Talent needs training, or it's a danger to yourself and everyone around you. Farmer or Lakewalker."

His tired mind brought up again the nightmare memory of Crane, the renegade Lakewalker who Barr had once helped put down, and his bandit gang with him. Which had for-sure shown young Barr that Lakewalker affinity with malices was no myth. "At least you've done nothing worse so far than beguile your horse."

"I didn't either magic Moon!" she shot back, sounding incensed as if at an accusation. Threatened? "He loves me!"

"It doesn't have to be one or t'other, you know," Barr pointed out mildly. "It can be both." Any applicability to Barr and her mother was not something he cared to suggest to her. Or think about. *Too late for that.*

She leaned against the horse, combing through the long mane with her fingers. A surly mumble: "Moon's the only one who ever did love me. Mama hates me, always did. Even before Edjer." She cast Barr a slightly poisonous glance, her face pale in the colorless light. "And now I know why, I guess."

He'd kept this knowledge in his pack for a dozen years, the edges wearing blunt with the abrasion of time and thought. Lily hadn't even held it for a dozen hours, fresh and cutting-sharp. *Patroller field-aid, eh.* Barr blew out his breath, sinking to a seat on the steps and dangling his hands between his knees. "If that were true, she could have handed you to me when you were two. Or thrown you away some other how. But she kept you. Took care of you." Though Bell might simply be one of those women who didn't know any other way to be than *taking care,* like Barr didn't know any other way to be than *patroller.* "Try this idea—that she was just afraid of you."

"Scared of *me?*" Lily's brow furrowed. "That I'd get powers?"

"Maybe some of that, but mostly because keeping the secret of your birth from Fid was a sore in her heart. Which your getting powers would reveal, true. She does love Fid in her way, I could see that, and there's no question he loves her. A gift she believes maybe she didn't deserve, but is deathly afraid of losing, and all her life that depends on it along-with."

Lily's face remained set, but by the churning in her ground he could tell she was thinking hard.

"That's a right heavy load for your mama to carry around for all those years. I'm not surprised she was rigid to you. But, you know, that's for her to fix. Not for you."

More mane-fiddling. "Reeve and Edjer...were always a spiteful misery to me. And she always took their parts, and never mine." She considered. "The littler ones are still too small to copy them much, but they're getting there."

This seemed pretty likely, really, that her siblings would pick up such cues and run with them, but not know why. "Was Fid more even-handed?"

"Yeah..." The admission was not so much reluctant as reflecting. "But you say he didn't know. Maybe..." Maybe Fid would have rejected her too, was she wondering? Barr wondered as well.

But he could just about watch as one more prop was pulled out from under her, as her spine slumped a little more. *Absent gods, I'm doing this all wrong.* "Holding secrets and lies like that isn't good. They blister in your hands like a coal. Not you, but her lie, was the secret waiting to burn down your mama's life."

Her glance flicked up. "And yours?"

Ouch. If he ever got a bow into her hands, she was going to be a hawk-eye, if that was a sample. "I think we've established that I was a fool when I was a youngling."

"Are you sorry I was ever born, too? Like Mama?" Her jaw set.

Ouch, ouch. He had no idea what to say to this, except the most truth he could muster. He flung out words as if over a cliff, with no guess as to where they would land. "I think... just maybe you have come upon me at the right time of my life. Because you are the most amazing person I have ever met, to show up and redeem so much old foolishness." His hands clenched each other.

She'd made it through all these past grueling days—the mortal slander, the flight, the painful disappointment of Glassforge, the strange journey through the woods with the stranger man, the malice sighting and the fight with the mud-man, the long sick ride, the devastating revelations at the end of it—without once giving in. But she crumpled now, sinking to the stoop as far from Barr as she could, bending over her knees, shoulders shaking like a woman with an ague. All she'd endured, and that one little random bit of praise stove in her hull and left her wrecked on the riverbank?

Maybe Barr shouldn't have been trying to take her anger away, if that was all that had been holding her upright.

She hadn't been abused, as far as he could tell, in the sense that she'd had food, had clothes, had a place to sleep safe and warm. She hadn't been worked harder than any other farm child, or camp child, when the labor of all hands, no matter how small, was needed to make sure all would survive the next winter, or the next malice. Was *praise-starved* a thing you could die of?

Just how long a winter famine had it been? It seemed she'd handed him the key to her, all unknowing, and it wouldn't even take magery. He wasn't sure he should ought'a have that much power.

"Don't...don't *do* that!" she mumbled to her knees.

Ah. Not so unknowing as all that. "Sorry. Porcupine." The nickname fell too aptly from his mouth to do anything but stick, and his lips twitched up. All fierce bristling spines curled around a soft, vulnerable underbelly? Yeah.

Her shoulders shook again, but in a different way. "Don't make me laugh like that," she snapped, still into her lap. "Makes me mad."

Good?

Moon moved over and lipped her hair, and she raised her face and stroked his soft nose. He snorted a light spray of horse slobber on her, which disgusted her not at all. She rubbed it off with the back of her hand, disguising the other silver tracks. Sniffed and straightened.

A slim figure was advancing in the moonlight; Barr recognized her from her ground before he could see her face.

"There you are, you bad thing!" the horse-girl chided, her tone not as irate as her words. "At least you didn't get far."

Lily blinked in brief bewilderment, then recognized, as Barr had, that the other girl was talking to Moon.

"I'm sorry, your"—a little ground flick, and she changed her address from Barr to Lily—"your horse got out. My word, that is the most beguiled beast I've ever seen. You might want to do something about that."

Barr put in, "Lily, this is Jena, one of our horse-girls, works at the patrol paddocks. Women run the river ferry, too. You'll have to see that come daylight. Night duty, is it, Jena?" The Tent Whiteheron girl must be, hm, sixteen by now?

"Hello, Barr, sir. They said you were back. Yes, all month." She yawned, and patted Moon's dappled haunch in a friendly way.

"And this is Miss Lily Mason"—*who owns Moon,* he could say, unexceptionably. "My daughter," he finished instead. "She owns Moon."

A startled ripple in Jena's ground was quickly eclipsed by what to her were more pressing concerns. "That is one pretty little horse you have, Lily!"

"Oh...thank you," said Lily faintly.

"But, um...maybe you could come with me to settle him? Or he's just like to be getting out again. Jumped right over the paddock fence, he did. A heavier horse couldn't have cleared it, I think."

"Good idea, Jena," said Barr, beginning to grin. "You can show Lily your work. But put shoes on first, Lily." Somewhere inside, Verel kept a keg of walking sticks of assorted lengths, but Barr was not inspired to go hunt it up. Boots. His boots would be a challenge right now, too.

After a hesitant look at him, Lily darted within, back in a moment with her own boots shoved on, pushing her nightshirt into her dirty trousers. "It's you who was taking care of Moon and Briar?" she asked Jena.

"They'd arrived before I come on night duty, but I was told all about them." Jena turned and waved her, and Moon, into her wake. The gelding, calming down in echo of his mistress, followed the girls amiably.

Barr should likely get up and escort them. "Make sure Lily gets back here all right," he called instead. "She doesn't know her way around the camp yet."

"Right, sir!"

"Do you take care of a lot of horses?" Lily's voice drifted through the moist night air.

"Oh, yes, Pearl Riffle's got nearly two hundred patrol horses, and about twenty-five broodmares. You've come at the right time of year—about half the new foals are born already, so darling...!"

Voices and figures faded away into the shadows.

The porch post was not all that comfortable a prop. He should hoist himself up and go back to bed. Maybe when Lily returned. Real soon now...

"...AKE UP. BA—YOU—JUST wake up!"

A hand was poking his shoulder. "Huh...?" Barr blinked haze from his eyes.

"You shouldn't fall asleep sitting all crooked like that," Lily said sternly. "I'm sure it's bad for your neck."

Still on the stoop, oh. "You're likely right." *Ow, gods.* Moving was a penance, yes indeed. He stretched and cracked the neck in question, the muffled popping making Lily recoil.

"Eew, don't do *that,* either! It sounds horrible!"

"Unh." Barr started to rise, then switched to using the post to pull himself up.

"...What should I call you anyways?" Lily went on, frowning at him. "I'm not going to call you Papa."

"No, that's Fid's title. He earned it. Didn't he."

A hunched sort of shrug of agreement. A small voice. "Yeah."

Which reminded Barr, they needed to get a courier letter off to Hackberry Corner soon, to assure the Masons that Lily was found safe. But not right this minute, gods. Verel had been right, blight him. Barr wasn't riding anywhere tomorrow...later this morning. A hint of steel was growing along the edge of the starry vault, and the moon was flirting with the western hills. Pale fog wisped above the river.

Barr drew a breath, which also hurt. "I think...given how complicated both our lives have got, we should keep one thing simple. Just call me Barr, like you have been."

"If you say so," Lily replied doubtfully.

"I do."

And then back inside, to stagger off to their respective beds. Again. Was Lily's ground less dark and curdled, now? The patrol paddocks had been a good distraction, maybe.

Barr wasn't sure he had any cause to feel so oddly heartened, but as he pulled the blessed sheet up and tried to find a position for his pillow that didn't catch on any prickly stitches, he had to allow he did.

⌒•⌒

"WELL," SAID A raspy voice. "Aren't you pretty this morning. Dancing with bears, were you?"

Barr pried open his eyes and stared through blear at the grizzled face of Fin Kingfisher, looming over him. Ah. Amma'd sent to roust him out last night—reserve patrol leader this rotation, right. It scarcely needed the sight of the deerskin parchment map rolled in his hand to tell Barr why he was the day's first visitor. Of course Fin would want an eyewitness report before he led his patrol off to deal with the malice. Pink dawn light was reflecting through the bunkroom window, muting the oil lamp Fin had set on the table. Over at the paddocks, the place would be bustling as people saddled up.

"Think that mud-man"—Barr heaved himself into a sitting position in his bunk, every muscle feeling like a rusty gate hinge—"might've been a wolverine. It was so underripe you could hardly tell, all slimy and slippery. And you think they stink when they're dry and fluffy." He rolled his shoulders and stretched his neck, and immediately regretted doing so. *Ow.*

"Guess you won't be riding out as a guide with us," said Fin, looking him over.

"I'd rather not..."

"No," said a firm voice. Maker Yina, bless her and keep her, stepped in to hand Barr a mug of hot, strong tea. He had to take it in both hands to keep it from slopping all over. "Verel's ordered camp rest for this one. You can't have him."

"You'd have to arm-wrestle Mother for him, and you'd lose," said another voice. Barr almost choked on the tea he was sluicing down his gullet, and looked up as another patroller leaned around Fin's shoulder: Barr's middle brother, Bay. Both men were geared up to ride out, so it was an easy guess he must be in Fin's patrol today. Bay shared the Foxbrush looks, average height and stocky, though with light brown hair to Barr's blond. In a sawed-off braid down his back today, no mourning knot, oh good. Courier letters from home, rare and sporadic, had reached Barr in Luthlia, but he'd been on the road quite a while. Things could happen while a man's back was turned. As he'd lately been reminded.

Bay's grin was crooked and confused. And worried. "I only just found out from the horse girls that you were back. Why didn't you come home last night?"

"We got in late, and then kept Verel busy for a while," Barr said evasively.

"You haven't busted another leg all to blight and gone, have you?" Because Bay, too, knew the walking wounded were routinely sent to their families' tents.

"Not this time, though I wrenched it pretty good dancing with that mud-man. I'll be hobbling around on a stick for a few days."

Yina nodded confirmation. "Some beautiful bruises, too, if you like purple."

"Report first, tent-kin reunion next," Fin cut in, unrolling the map across Barr's sheeted lap. "Where exactly did you find this sessile—it was a sessile, right?—and how far along was it?"

Barr nodded, and launched into the necessary descriptions: location as exactly as he could describe it, number and ripeness of the mud-men pots, his estimate, pretty shrewd by now, of the probable time till the malice's first molt. For all his attempts to hew to just the facts, it soon became apparent he hadn't been riding alone, nor heading for home.

Making up some tarradiddle to send them on their way in temporary ignorance of Lily was possible but pointless, Barr figured. And, blight it, he was proud of how well Lily had done with her first mud-man, leaving aside that little lapse about *stay with the horses.* Just who his companion and charge had been, and how he'd acquired her, came out necessarily along with the brag.

Bay looked appalled. Fin didn't look like anything much, which was Fin's usual expression when he was cogitating. Fin had been on the fence about the use of farmer-patrollers, Barr recalled, not enthusiastic but willing to give the scheme a fair shake. Bay's response was more personal. Or familial.

"I thought the horse girls just had hold of some garbled gossip!" said Bay. "I'd say *Tell me it isn't so,* but I s'ppose I should know you better by now. Farmer women, Barr, you blighted fool! Absent gods, does Amma know?"

"She will soon as she gets time today, I expect."

"'Cause she'll rip you up one side and down the other for that!"

"It was fifteen years ago, Bay. Even Amma will realize it's a bit late." *And I never did anything like it again* was a plea best saved for Amma, Barr figured; that wasn't Bay's main concern.

"You know she was groomin' you for patrol leader. If we ever got you back alive from Luthlia, that is, which by some wonderment it looks like we did. How could you go and mess that chance up?" It wasn't clear if Bay's red-faced frustration was on Barr's behalf, or his own.

"Well, that's not my first concern anymore." *And I'd be every bit the blight you've always thought me if it were.* His new preoccupation with Lily was a strange and awkward feeling, as though his skin had been stretched over two people, not one.

"And how d'you think Mama and Dad are going to take this? Mama's passed the last two years dreading every courier that rode in from the north, afraid you'd be brought back as nothing but the bits of a spent primed knife."

Stung, Barr returned, "Well, she should ought'a be glad to have me back breathing with a bonus, then!"

"How you rate some half-farmer bastard as a bonus— only you, Barr! Absent *gods* you haven't changed. Still a chirping embarrassment to the tent."

Barr had pulled in his ground tight upon awaking to this delegation, by reflex. So it wasn't till he glimpsed the movement of faded cloth in the doorway that he realized the debate had another audience. Nightshirt and bare feet, so Lily must have been drawn out of bed by the raised voices. How long had she been standing there listening?

Fin followed his glance, eyes narrowing. "This your farmer...girl, then?"

Uncertainly, Lily sidled into the room, edging nearer to Yina. Yina, with a medicine maker's acuity, stepped up behind her and put both hands on her shoulders. With this support silently backing her, Lily gulped and said, "Barr, are you, um, all right?" She shot a scowl at Bay.

Barr cleared his throat. "Oh, sure."

Fin turned toward her; she flinched back, but he only said, "Miss, ah, Mason, is it? I purely would appreciate it if you could give me your tale of the malice sighting yesterday. Not to waste a second eyewitness, since I can get one."

"This is Fin Kingfisher, Lily," Yina put in. "It's going to be his job to lead his patrol out today to put down that malice that you and Barr found."

"With one of those magic knives?"

"Yes, a patrol always carries a few primed knives, though there are never enough to go around," said Yina. "So it would help him to know everything you saw."

"...Everything?"

"About the malice and the mud-men. That's the only part he needs."

"I see." Under Yina's encouraging grip, Lily swallowed and launched into her account, the same events but differently angled, starting with what had to her been

Barr's inexplicable abandonment of her on the trail with the horses and her growing anxiety. All right, maybe he should have said something more, but he hadn't wanted to scare her. The blank, it seemed, had just left more room for her imagination to run wild, the opposite of his intention. Barr's quick, brutal tangle with the mud-man had apparently exceeded her imaginings, oops. Her voice, which had been surprisingly steady under Fin's gimlet gaze, shook in the memory of that part, her word-picture of Barr staggering around bleeding unnecessarily gruesome, Barr thought. Though certainly vivid. Her description of the sessile malice and its position was clear and accurate, for such a short glimpse, the only thing Fin cross-questioned her about.

"Right," said Fin, easing back less vulture-like when it was apparent there were no more useful details to be extracted. "I'll be on my way, then. Barr, welcome home, and, ah...half a *mile* off the trail, you say?"

"And some change. Up the ravine."

"Interestin'." Fin pursed his lips.

"It should be pretty straightforward," Barr offered, uneasy under this considering gaze. "As such things go."

"Yeah, but Amma's stuck me with a tail of her younglings, to give them a chance to see their first malice. It's going to make for a blighted parade. Bay, you follow on. We won't be waiting for you."

"Yes, sir." Bay nodded at this tacit, if limited, permission to finish their reunion. Barr wasn't sure if either Foxbrush brother was exactly grateful. With a vague salute to Lily and Yina, Fin strode out, more expressionless than ever.

Barr motioned Lily to his bedside; she approached warily. "Lily, this here's my older brother, your uncle Bay. So sorry about that."

"Hey," Bay objected. He and Lily frowned at each other in matching dismay. Confronted with that direct blue stare, Bay hunched his shoulders in discomfort. Yina made herself unobtrusive, muting her ground to a shadow and leaning against the wall by the door.

Lily raised her chin. "You were yellin' at Barr." Her tone of accusation, as though this were an offense, quite charmed Barr. Was she setting out to *defend* him?

Bay waved this away. "We been yellin' at him for years. It doesn't have any effect."

She blinked in confusion. "Well, it's…still not nice."

Was there, beneath her bristle, a hint of real fear? If Barr was her only prop here, she must be wondering how weak a reed she had to rely on.

Bay didn't answer this, but turned to Barr. Or on Barr. "You know we're *still* having to talk young flatties out of wearing pots on their heads when they meet with us? There were a couple down at the ferry just last week."

"Really?" said Barr, diverted. Yina bit back a smile.

"What?" said Lily, confused by this sudden turn onto camp history.

Bay jerked his head toward his brother. "It was Barr's most famous tarradiddle, back when he and his partner

Remo were raising trouble all around the Riffle. They persuaded a gang of flatboat men hung up waiting for the river to rise that they could protect themselves from Lakewalker magics by wearing iron helmets, like the soldiers in the old broken statues, except nobody had any iron helmets. So they used the nearest things they had to hand. Amma and the ferry boss were so mad at you two. So were the flatties who figured it out."

Barr remembered that part. Speaking of spectacular bruises. "Well, at least you'd hope it would teach farmers not to believe every lie they hear about Lakewalkers."

"Not so's you'd notice," sighed Bay.

"We didn't know it would get down the whole river!" Barr protested. He made a face. "Or last so long."

"How long ago was this?" asked Lily.

"Ten…no, thirteen years back," said Bay. "You'd think you would've learned your lesson about joking around, Barr."

"Well, you told *me* those scary lies about groundsense making you see ghosts. And that thing about the bloodsucking water monster. 'Slop, slop, its webbed claws go as it climbs the riverbank, dripping and snuffling for you,'" he quoted in an eerie quaver, waving his hands fin-fashion. "Kept me awake at nights for *months.*"

"You were twelve," said Bay, defensively.

"Yes, that was the problem!"

Lily's lips screwed up. "Just how long have you two been having this argument, anyway?"

"Twenty…years?" Barr worked it out.

"Yeah, we're probably not going to put it to bed this morning," allowed Bay.

The new argument, over farmer women and what Barr should not have been doing with them, had died abruptly when Lily's arrival in the room had been noticed. Bay was not by any means a subtle man—it wasn't a Foxbrush trait—but Barr had caught that care with a dry appreciation. Seemed his brother wasn't a complete blight, these days. Least not all the time.

"But Fin's going to be pissed with me if I don't catch up before the patrol rides out," Bay continued. "What you should do this morning, Barr, if you can hobble that far, is to get your tail up to the tent. Nobody there knows you're back yet, but word'll get around soon. You might want to get your word in first." He cast a shrewd glance at Lily.

"Given how garbled camp—or river—gossip can get, I suppose that's true," Barr admitted reluctantly. Flatties wearing their cookpots on their heads being only one case in point. "Yeah, go have a nice ride." He couldn't resist adding, in a kindly tone, "It's about time you got a malice kill to your name."

Bay, grimacing, paused at the door to ask, "How many did you get in Luthlia?"

"With my patrols? Eight."

"In two years. Absent gods."

"Plus one sessile all by myself on my way home, that I ran across in north Raintree," Barr continued cheerily. "So, nine. And the two we took out on the Tripoint Trace that time, comes to eleven. And the one we found yesterday. I guess I'll make you a present of that one."

Bay made a rude gesture and took himself off, laughing blackly.

Barr sank back against his bunk's headboard, his brief amusement evaporating as he took in Lily's flummoxed expression. He coughed, regretted it, and came up with, "Just how much of that argument did you hear, Lily?"

She shrugged. "I came in when your brother was talking about the gossiping horse girls."

"Oh." All the worst of it, then. *Ouch.*

"Was that true?" Her voice was hunched and small. She was going to master groundshielding in no time, at this rate. "Are you going to be punished because of me?"

"I've never been punished for anyone but me, trust me on that. Though I have to say as how not being promoted to patrol leader might actually be a reward. Thankless job. Another job that isn't mine is camp captain, who's the one who has to decide such things. That plate is all Amma's, and I don't want it, either. I just patrol where and when I'm told all the same. A simple life, but it suits me."

She frowned at him in suspicion. "Are you tarradiddling me?"

A muffled snort from Yina, which Barr overrode with, "Not much, no. But any decision that's above my rank is definitely above yours, so it's a waste of sweat to worry about it." He eyed her back. "Now what's churning around in your head?" And her ground.

An uncertain breath. "It's just...nothing here's what I expected."

"Well," said Barr heartily, hoisting his legs out of the bunk and sitting up, "how dull would that be?" The room only swayed a little. "Now, if Maker Yina here hasn't hidden our clothes so's we can't leave, I suppose we should get dressed and take ourselves over to Tent Foxbrush."

"It's no use hiding patrollers' clothes to keep them in bed," said Yina. "They'd just crawl off naked. But yes, we'd appreciate that. Patients could start trickling in any time, and I'd be better use putting a ground reinforcement in those stitches than rustling your breakfasts. Verel would be peeved if I let a dirty infection get started. Fetch a walking stick out of the keg, and Quen can bring your saddlebags along in a barrow."

This brisk program was carried out. Soon enough, they were trudging, or in Barr's case limping, across the face of the hill toward his family's tent-cluster. Quen came after, trundling the laden barrow. Barr made sure to point out to Lily the ferry serving the old straight road, just downriver, the barge halfway across with a load of travelers, horses, and a wagon. The clank of the capstan winding and unwinding the cable carried faintly on the damp morning air. The sky to the west was graying out; rain later.

"Camp women run the ferry," Barr said, "which is the camp's best source of steady cash. As well as take care of our mounts." Lily craned her neck to take in the patrol paddocks downslope, dotted with horses. She seemed to ease when she spied Moon, head down cropping grass, evidently unbullied by his new pasture mates.

"There are lots of camp chores Lakewalker women do besides patrol," Barr went on, invitingly. "Really, everything you'd do on a farm, plus everything folks contribute to support our patrols in the field."

"Farm?" Lily looked around, plainly puzzled.

"There are fields up over the ridge, and the pastures for the broodmares and the resting mounts." The kitchen gardens, chicken pens, blossoming fruit and nut trees, and beehives were scattered along the slope around the kin-tents, self-explanatory. "Besides fishing, we also trade with the rivermen, despite some folks disapproving of getting dependent. Sell them things we make better, though the river-town crafters are getting blighted clever these days. The towns are growing." *Malice bait,* said some, not without just cause, but that was another argument.

He wasn't sure what Lily was making of his hints, but she did say, "So it's not just ridin' around."

"Not hardly. Though for all the work, camps don't ever get much ahead. On the other hand, the world hasn't got eaten." *Yet.* "That dead gray blight you saw yesterday will take decades to heal. Centuries, or maybe never, for the huge old disasters like the Western Levels."

"Which you've seen…"

He wondered what she was picturing now. "Aye."

Lily frowned at her moving feet. "Is every Lakewalker we meet going to be able to tell how we're related?"

"Mm, generally. It takes someone with keen ground-sense who's paying attention to work it out exactly."

And then the Foxbrush kin tents hove into view. A shudder of anticipation, like a starving man scenting a meal, or an exhausted man confronted with a soft bed, shook Barr. He tried to imagine what his home looked like to Lily's stranger-eyes. A half-circle of log cabins with leather flaps hung across their fronts; a central fire pit; a scattering of seats made from upended cut logs. Pretty crude, compared to her farmhouse in Hackberry Corner. Before it had burned down. But the fruit trees were looking healthy, and he could hear the murmur of his sister's prized bees in their hives up-slope among them. The low smokehouse, leaking an aromatic haze, would be familiar anywhere. Unfamiliar even to his eyes was the add-on at the side of the ever-more-sprawling main tent, its timbers raw and bright. And was that a spanking new *pump shed* where the old well had been? *Ooh.*

"Here we are," Barr announced. *Here we go.* Barely seeming aware of the gesture, Lily grasped his hand. Her fingers felt small and cold. He returned the grip, faking reassurance, entirely too aware of entirely too much.

Barr drew in a great lungful of Grace River valley air, and bellowed, "Good morning, Tent Foxbrush! You'd better have left us some breakfast!"

THE TENT FLAP twitched back, and his eldest sister Shirri stuck her head out, eyes widening and jaw dropping in a gratifying fashion. "Mama!" she shouted over her shoulder. "It's Barr!"

A maternal shriek from inside was followed in a moment by Kiska Foxbrush herself, pelting past. "It is! *Barr!* We've been waiting and waiting!" Some more anxiously than others, clearly, but even Shirri, leaning on the doorjamb, smiled at him.

His mother's braided gold hair might have a touch more silver in it, but the strength of her hug was in no wise enfeebled. It wasn't just for duty that Barr hugged her back, though he did not tease by lifting her off her feet as he'd sometimes done after reaching his full man's size. Though only because yesterday's bruises had stiffened up more than his short hobble across camp could amend, *ouch.* "Hey, hey! When have I never?"

"We thought sure some Luthlian girl would snag you for her tent, and all we could hope for was that she might be a better letter-writer than you."

The other reasons a tent-child might not come back from an exchange patrol were left unspoken, as one did. "Naw. Luthlian girls are warm, but the winters are way too cold." Barr mimed a shudder.

Her hand—had it been that gnarled before?—rose to his neck. "What's this, then? Verel's sewing, I daresay. That's never a souvenir from Luthlia."

"No, that was my welcome-home to Pearl Riffle territory, just yesterday. We ran across a sessile and a mud-man—not a day's ride north of camp, if you can believe it."

"So that's what Bay rode out for this morning," said Shirri, huffing an astonished laugh. "Your trail luck! I swear you must bait them, Barr!"

He tapped his forehead and bragged, "Groundsense. It's up to over half a mile now."

"Aha. I knew you weren't done growing!" his mama said proudly. She stepped back at last, her gaze and unfurling groundsense swinging to Lily, who'd been watching this welcome wide-eyed. Barr braced himself. "Is this young lady...another souvenir of Luthlia?" his mama began uncertainly. "No..." Her lips thinned in confusion as she took in the details. Kiska was patroller herself, not maker, but he didn't doubt her perceptions on this score would be as keen as Verel's.

Barr stood straight on his stick and wrapped his free arm around Lily's cringing shoulders. "This here's Miss Lily Mason of Hackberry Corner. My daughter. She's fourteen."

Shirri took in the implications and emitted a faint, familiar wail: "Oh, *Baarrr*."

Kiska Foxbrush stared at Lily in stillness for a moment, perhaps doing the arithmetic, plus a number of other calculations, in her head. But she only bit her lip, then said, "Indeed. And was this a surprise to you, too, Miss Lily Mason?"

Lily stared back at this unexpected grandmother and gulped, "Yes, ma'am."

"I see." The narrow blue eyes were all for Barr, now. "And how long have you known?"

He shrugged uncomfortably. "About twelve years. But that she'd grow Lakewalker, just since I swung by Hackberry Corner on my way home last week."

"Huh." A contemplative pause, while Barr held his breath. And then, "Breakfast, eh? Long rides leave a patroller hungry. A thousand miles worth, is it? You two'd better come inside. Shirri, get your youngsters to put up the flap."

Barr motioned Quen to unload their bags from the barrow, releasing him to return to the medicine tent. He gave Lily's stiff shoulders another encouraging squeeze and led her into Tent Foxbrush. "It's not a bear's den," he whispered.

"You sure?" she murmured back.

He thought of his formidable grandmother Nura Foxbrush, long-time tent matriarch, and lied, "Yep." And where was she, this morning? A furtive check with his groundsense did not find her in the rambling, connected clutch of cabins that was the main kin tent.

Several of the old parchment-covered windows had been replaced with glass, brightening the big main room that was kitchen and dining hall and workroom together. The space lightened further as, under Shirri's direction, her two eldest children lifted the heavy tent flap on its poles to create an awning half the width of the cabin. Spring air wafted in, replacing the night's fug of cooking and leatherwork and too many people.

Further questions and comments were, thankfully, shelved for a time as the two adult women bustled about the routine of finding a fast meal. Between commands from the cooks, Shirri's children, a few years younger than Lily and caught between curiosity and shyness, stared at their strange new cousin. Raki and Azio were both dark-haired and whippy like their father, Barr's senior tent-brother from north Raintree, breaking the run of sturdy blonds in the Foxbrush kin-hold. Their grounds were noisy and unshielded, as open as a meadow, the ordinary inevitable chaos of children; confused but not hostile, so all right so far.

Lily's was not quite as open, but every adult Lakewalker present could read her dark anxiety, as if her tight, strained stance and thin voice were not hint enough. No one here, Barr thought with relief, was inclined to be mean to her, however awkward they found her presence. And it seemed Barr was partially spared by his welcome-home status, which, if he'd planned it, would have been right clever of him.

They settled as directed on either side of a long table not much different from the one in the Tamaracks' farm kitchen. No iron cookstove here, though, just the hearth and spark-spitting fireplace. If Tent Foxbrush had advanced to a pump shed and window glass, it couldn't just be camp conservatism holding up progress, so the lack was more likely due to a flat tent-purse. Barr wondered if he could do anything about that. He was afraid the place looked pretty crude to Lily's eyes, used to less harried and hurried farmer craftsmanship. Or was it his own eyes that had changed?

Lily eased a trifle in surprise as a small mountain of food was plunked down in front of them: ham, eggs fried in drippings, smoked venison, dried apple and plum and plunkin not flavored with saddlebag, abundant hot sassafras tea, corncakes, hard cheese and goat cheese, and a big pot of Shirri's good honey. Barr elected not to explain that this was not some special hello-there feast, just the provender normally slung in front of famished, tired patrollers. His aches and Lily's tension kept them from actually wolfing it, though he was pleased to see her appetite revive and posture unfold with each new bite.

He caught his mama, too, checking the effect of her cooking on Lily, and nodding in satisfaction. Her narrow-eyed look at him grew a trifle grim, though. He made a helpless hand gesture out of sight of Lily, *Later.* Mama sniffed.

Between bites, he managed to decant the immediate tale of the malice-sighting and their tangle with the mud-man. Even Lily contributed a cautious mite, if mainly descriptions of Barr not at his best. He thought it pushed up her standing in his mother's eyes, at least, and he didn't even have to stretch the truth.

When Lily volunteered to help with the washing-up, Shirri let her; ah, another chink in the Foxbrush walls. It was clear enough the Foxbrush women wanted more words with him, and not in front of Lily, which was both good and ominous. At least they'd had the charity not to blame Lily for her own existence, but that left only one target.

"Well." Barr sluiced down the last of his tea and wiped his lips. "I'll just put my bags away, then." He had a few real souvenirs from Luthlia to unpack, as well.

"Ah," said his mother. "Azio has your bunk now, since he graduated from the truckle. I guess you can use Bay's bunk until he gets back."

"Oh." He hesitated. "And for Lily?"

The female gazes upon him were a mix of calculating and worried. Shirri allowed, "We can fix up a bedroll for her in the girls' room, for now."

His mother went on, "We've some catching up to do. It's been quite a while since our last letter."

No one was wearing new mourning knots, Barr reminded himself.

"Raki," Shirri called, "why don't you show Lily around the camp a bit. It looks to rain later on."

Obviously getting her out of the way so's the grownups could talk frankly. A good idea? Not? He decided to back this: "Yeah, she's only seen the patroller stables and the medicine tent, so far. And the outside of patrol headquarters, and that after dark."

Shirri raised her eyebrows and lowered her voice. "Aye? And what does Amma think of all this?"

"Hnh."

But Raki seemed to cotton to the idea of being appointed trailmaster, bouncing up and instantly tossing out a few ideas for a tour, and absent gods where did youngsters get so much *energy*? After a glance at Barr for, he hoped, permission and not rescue, Lily followed Raki out.

Her voice, wary but curious, wafted back, "Are you Shirri—Aunt Shirri's daughter, then?"

"Yep. I'm oldest, so I'll be tent-heiress someday."

"So we're first cousins, I guess." Cousins were not a novelty in Lily's world, nor in Raki's, but surprise new cousins had to be equally a challenge to both. Though only one of them was on her home ground. And wasn't it odd to reflect that the youngest child of his generation, himself, had fathered the oldest child of the next?

Raki went on, with a rather dramatic hush, "Are you really a *farmer?*"

A hesitation. "I always thought I was…"

Their footsteps faded.

Barr went to stow his saddlebags. The space underneath Bay's bunk was packed with its owner's belongings, so he ended up dumping his gear at the foot, leaving the top of Bay's trunk for laying things out. Lightly, like a visitor at an inn. He came back to the main room to find Azio had evidently been sent as a runner to find his grandmother Nura, because the three Foxbrush women were now seated around the end of the table, catching up the news in low murmurs. The descending generations of faces all swung toward him as he entered.

There was this for it; he'd only have to tell the whole tale once, again. He took a seat below his mother, as potentially a better shield than Shirri. She shoved a fresh mug of tea his way, half welcome, half threat, *You'd better not stop talking.*

"Well," said his grandmother, chief judge of this panel, "make no doubt I'm glad to have you back in one piece, Barr." Yeah, he wouldn't have figured that from her dubious tone, so perhaps it needed saying. "But I think you'd bet-ter start this story at the beginning. About fifteen years ago, you say?"

Barr sighed. *I was eighteen...* He was sure they all remembered. A bit woodenly, he unloaded it all. The detail that he'd not just seduced but actively beguiled Bluebell went over just about as well as he'd expected. Since he'd had his head thoroughly washed for that at the time by Remo, and then Dag and Fawn, them wanting to do it all over again seemed redundant, but he supposed the Foxbrush women had to get it out of their systems. He hunkered down and endured.

At least the Lakewalker custom of training every youth to patrolling, regardless of what tasks they took up after, meant that every one of the women at the table had been out in the wider world as he had, seen the great duty through her own eyes. Felt the grueling discomfort of the endless trail in all weathers, the itch and scrape of having to work with the same people with no escape for week after week, the long boredom of a search repeated over and over with no results. Not that you'd *want* a malice, but the horror of missing one that was actually there was always enough to keep everyone on edge, bleeding into each other.

And each of the women also knew that it was not unknown for a passing female Lakewalker to sometimes beguile a cute farmer lad, a transgression equally fiercely frowned-upon if for slightly different reasons. At least farmer lads couldn't get pregnant, but Barr had been around the hinterlands enough by now to see how their lives could be wrecked in subtler ways. *Keep it buttoned up* wasn't near as arbitrary a demand as it seemed to youngsters when they were just unbuttoning it in the first place, and he winced for his younger self.

Barr had the wits to let the tongue-lashings run down on their own before putting in, "And I agree with you. It's not even an argument anymore. But it wasn't Bluebell that changed my mind. It was that blighted monster Crane, running his bandit gang down the river those years back. That's where I saw what unrestrained Lakewalker powers could *really* do to farmers, driven by active cruelty and not just youthful spirits. I never want to help bury that many bodies again."

His grandmother, at least, nodded understanding. Shirri stirred and frowned. Mama clasped her hands and rested her mouth on them.

"Which brings me around again to Lily. She has the beginnings of ground control, and some range already, though I don't know yet if that will top out to full patroller. She's already beguiled her horse, not on purpose. But it wouldn't take much for her to figure out how to do it to other animals, and from there it's a step to people. Verel says she likely has enough affinity to share, someday." Barr stifled his twinge at that thought. "She *can't* be let go back to her farm, or anywhere else, untrained. Not that she wants to, and that's another whole tale. She can only get what she needs at a camp. Here or elsewhere." He let that last hint sit out, there on the table.

His mama lifted her chin. "And that brings me to another question. How in the world did you persuade her farmer family to let her go off with you?" The hint of a suspicion that Barr might still be using illicit powers on farmers was galling. It was only for mortal emergencies, he *understood* that.

"That," he sighed, "is the other whole tale. She'd run off from her farm on her own a few days before I got there. On an unrelated matter. Well...mostly unrelated," he allowed. Blight, he really had to get that letter on its way back to Fid and Bluebell, didn't he...

And then it was time to unload Lily's side of the story, as far as he knew it: the family secrets, the fire, the false accusations, the flight, the finding. At least his judges took it in with the seriousness he thought it deserved, frowns deepening all around at each added complication. Not his wounds, to be sure, but it would be downright cruel to make Lily bare it all herself to a table full of untrusted strangers. If he was to get what he wanted out of the Foxbrush women for Lily, he couldn't be leaving holes in the road to break legs later. Because he'd been learning some hard lessons about that, this past week.

His mama rubbed her jaw. "Seems the girl's had quite a time of it. There's no help for it for the moment, but news you likely hadn't got yet is that Toshi is getting string-bound next month. We'd figured to give the girls' room over to her and her young man."

A new tent-brother, moving in? Barr supposed it was an inevitability, and not before time. He wondered if his middle sister Toshi had managed to get pregnant yet, a duty her tent-kin had been hinting her toward since before Barr had left for Luthlia. To the point she'd got pretty prickly about it, since it evidently wasn't for lack of trying. Too bad they couldn't transplant some of whatever magic Bluebell had… "Who'd she pick?"

"Tona Sunfish. Seems to be a nice, steady fellow, what we've seen of him so far."

"Don't know him…?"

"He's a patroller out of Cub Run Camp. They met when she was exchanging down that way. A temporary lend for them being short-handed."

Not unusual, for neighboring camps to share such help; Cub Run covered a territory across the Grace upriver. "Doesn't sound like Cub Run came out ahead, then."

His grandmother grinned, fox-like. "Their loss, our gain."

"Any sign of Bay being taken off your hands?"

A glum silence spread around the table. Shirri sighed, "He's still not over Hana, I think."

A Pearl Riffle ferry girl Bay'd fancied for years, drowned in a bad spring flood just as he was fixing to join her tent. She hadn't even had a chance to share. Not every mortal hazard a Lakewalker faced was out on patrol, yet coming home to such news seemed a wrench and a wrongness, as if the world had flipped over topside-to. Bay didn't talk about it.

His mother eyed Barr. "I feel sorry enough for your Miss Lily, but have you quite thought through what bringing her back to camp like this is going to do for your own chances of getting string-bound? You'd just about lived down your reputation as a wild lad, and now this."

I hadn't meant to bring her here at all. Barr shifted uneasily. "I thought girls liked me well enough."

"You made 'em laugh, I'll grant. That's not the same thing as being reliable enough for one to pack home to her tent."

Pricked, Barr replied, "What patroller ever is, when he or she rides out?"

"Leaving aside all your japes and jokes and crazy starts," said Shirri, "I don't know another patroller that's half the malice-bait as you seem to be. Sector Six, really!"

Barr offered, after a moment's thought, "Dag."

A general, conceding silence. Barr's tent-kin didn't dislike Dag, insofar as they'd met him, but Barr suspected they still blamed him for the half-year-long unauthorized scarper to the sea, when they weren't blaming Remo or, more cogently, Barr himself. Desertion, or apparent desertion: that was another old grudge on his head, right up there with that horrible night he'd accidentally got Remo's new primed knife broke. Nobody talked about that one, either, the way nobody talked about Bay's girl Hana to him: a silence that grieved too much to poke at. Not that there hadn't been plenty said at the time. Maybe they'd all learned their lessons about saying too much, back then.

"Speaking of, where's Dad?" Barr asked.

"Running patrol in Sector Three," Kiska replied. "They should be back soon, though."

One of the close-in sectors; Barr's father was likely training young patrollers, a task that usually brought him home
in a ruffled state of mind. Wonderful; Barr'd get to get his
head washed *all over again,* again.

His grandmother leaned back in her seat and crossed
her arms, studying him. Giving nothing away. "So just
what exactly were you trying to get, bringing that girl
home?"

"Breakfast," he answered honestly, controlling his irri-
tation. "For which I thank you." But it wasn't an unfair
question, for all that his life had been tumbled tail over
teakettle worse'n that mud-man had rolled him down the
ravine yesterday. Blight, had it only been one day since
they'd found that sessile?

The conviction was creeping up on him, hour by hour: if
what Lily needed most was to learn how to be a Lakewalker,
and it was plain to him she did, she could learn it best how
every other Lakewalker did, embedded in a camp, in a tent.
And his best chance—no, her best chance—could well be
this tent right here.

So giving in to his temper—or, even more spineless, his
embarrassment—by threatening they were going to ride
off to Clearcreek, or Luthlia, or any other such ultimatum
or taking-of-offense, was exactly the wrong way of going
about it. Even if he won such an arm-wrestle with his tent-
kin, grudging acceptance wasn't going to be good enough.
Not for Lily, wounded porcupine that she was. He had to
gain more whole-hearted support for her. Somehow.

Hunting tactics seemed not a very useful guide, nor fishing, neither. Maybe this had to be more like gardening, planting the seed and waiting, not quite helplessly, for something good to grow out of its inner potential. You could weed and water, and not tread on the new leaves, but you couldn't force anything. Very farmerish; how apt.

In which case, what he most needed to solve this dilemma was not fiercer argumentation, but patience and time. And, perhaps, Lily herself. Seed of her own future. Or, wait, didn't lilies grow from bulbs? *Stop thinking, Barr, you're going to hurt yourself.*

But in his younger days, he had perfected slithering-out. Was there such a thing as slithering-*in?*

"Verel's put me on camp rest anyway," he declared. *Bless his little black heart.* "We can't go anywhere else for a while."

"Well," said his grandmother, frowning, "nobody's arguing with Verel."

Shirri's toddler woke up and wailed from the trundle in the next room, and the inquest broke up in a flurry of household chores. Barr dutifully admired his squirming nephew, the latest addition to Tent Foxbrush, and as reward, or punishment, was set to keep him from vigorously trying to kill himself in novel ways while his mother went out to deal with her bees. Wheezing a bit, Barr wondered how this was classed as a *light* duty, suitable for a convalescent. "No, kid, we don't *eat* leather scraps. And not awls either, good grief... No, nor candles, though I don't suppose beeswax would poison you..."

His grandmother, passing through with an armload of roving to spin up for some future shirt or saddle blanket, paused to watch this harried negotiation. "Huh. It's a rough road your farmer girl's rid down, Barr, but don't go thinking you can just dump your pack on Shirri and run off. She's carrying load enough right now. She had two more miscarriages while you were gone, you know."

Barr winced. "Her letters didn't say."

She puffed out a dry breath. "They wouldn't. You were in *Luthlia*. We figured you needed to keep your whole mind on the task in front of you, up there."

"Luthlia's really not that different from camps in Oleana, three seasons out of four." Barr reflected. "Poorer, maybe, but they take being able to move camp at a moment's notice a lot more seriously. Their patrol's more...more strained than here, though. Far more strained than any Lakewalker enclave I saw south of the Barrens."

"I daresay." She contemplated him for a moment. "For all that Amma complains about what she calls your *joy-jaunts*, your travels have been the making of you, I think."

Barr blinked, but even he couldn't work this out for a criticism. Glory be. "I think so, too." His mouth tweaked up. "Maybe we should send Bay to Luthlia, next. One of the girls up there might collect him."

"They didn't take you. And you're cuter'n him."

"Yeah, well... I guess I made it too plain I meant to come home, after."

Her gaze sharpened. "Because of Lily?"

He wouldn't have said so out loud, but… "Maybe some."

"Hm." She stumped away to collect her spindle.

HAVING THANKFULLY TRADED off the toddler, Barr had been given a sit-down chore outside at the smaller fire pit, tending to a kettle of Shirri's wax, melting and cleaning it. The slow-moving sky had congealed into a cool mist threatening rain when Lily and Raki came tromping back. Raki was called inside by her mother, no doubt for her next chore; Lily, after a lurch in her wake, came instead over to Barr's side.

"So what all did you see?" he asked amiably.

"We went down by the river and watched where they were building narrow-boats. One woman was carving paddles, and let us both try with scraps. And then we stopped at a, a tent-cabin, where some people were practicing music. I didn't know Lakewalkers did that."

"Out on patrol we have to make our own entertainment, yes. Though only with little instruments we can tuck in saddlebags. There's a lot of songs. Most morose, some funny. Some both, but you have to know patroller humor."

She twisted her lips, as if this explained something. "Then we went over the ridge and saw the broodmare pastures, and the foals, and the fields. People were planting. And then back up, and saw across the river to your ferry landing, and all the way down past the rapids to Pearl Bend—I didn't realize there was a farmer town practically next door to you!" Her eyes were full of new; it made them brighter. *Good.*

"River town, really. The river is like its own hinterland. The Bend has a ferry of their own at the foot of the Riffle, as we have the one at the head. They deal more with boat ladings, folks portaging loads around the bad stretch. Our ferry is smack on the old straight road, serves folks going overland. Although that's a bonus for us. Really, we maintain it to be sure patrols can get across if needed."

"Is everything here about patrols, in the end?"

Her questions were growing shrewder every day, huh. Or maybe every hour. "Pretty much."

At his gesture, she seated herself on the sawn-off log beside him, not uncompanionably. Barr, it seemed, had now been promoted to the rank of her familiar anchor in a sea of strangeness, if only for want of her horse. Lily waved toward the straggle of kin Foxbrush tents beyond the main tent. "Raki claims those are all your relatives, too?"

"Ayup. My grandmother Nura is senior, tent-head, but those cabins stuck together on the end are for her younger sister, um, my great-aunt, and her two daughters, and their string-bound fellows—husbands, you would say, though I count them as tent-brothers, and their youngsters. And the one in the middle is my mother's sister, and her three girls, and their two partners so far, and their kids."

"That's...are they all Foxbrushes?"

"Yeah, there must be rising forty of us, last I counted. The generations get a bit skewed, so we just call them all cousins or aunts." He added after a moment, "My oldest brother married out to another camp years ago. So have most of the other fellows I grew up with. Their youngsters would be your cousins, too, though they don't count as Foxbrushes. But we don't see them often."

She absorbed this. "What do you do when it gets to be too much? All you Lakewalkers thrown in together. You said you didn't like crowds." She frowned, perhaps in memory of her bad night in Glassforge.

"Well, there's groundshielding." Barr grinned. "When even that's not enough anymore, we go patrollin'. Or hunting. Or fishing on the river. Or go up to the woods and shoot arrows into innocent trees."

"Hard on the poor trees."

"Can be, yeah."

Barr leaned over and stirred the melted wax in the hot water. The bee-bits were mostly falling to the bottom, good. "Almost ready to let cool. We'll fish out the wax when it hardens, save it for the next batch of candles, and run the water through a cheesecloth and use for sweet tea. A two-handed job, if you'll lend one."

"Sure." She bent over and picked up the little peg-studded board that he'd leaned against his log. "Are you braiding candlewick string?"

"Ayup. Care to try your hand?"

"We do this the same at home. I know how." Pensively, she gathered up the cotton plies and began to crisscross them.

"Did those Foxbrush women give you a hard time about me?" Her sideways glance tried to be opaque, and failed.

"The scars will heal." He smirked, inviting her to be amused at his expense, hoping she wouldn't take criticism of Barr as censure of herself. "Upshot was, we both have a place to sleep tonight dry and warm. It'll do for a start. I'm safe till my stitches come out, for sure." Which were itching again; he dutifully did not scratch, *rgh.*

He let Lily ease into the maybe-comforting familiar task for a few minutes, her fingers flicking, then he stirred the wax-water again and sighed. "There is one chore this afternoon we can't put off." *Much as I would like to.* "We need to write a letter for a Lakewalker courier to carry to your folks in Hackberry Corner, let them know you're found safe. Thing is, I'm not sure what all else to say. Your mama and aunt Iris both know you're half Lakewalker, but no one else seemed to. And neither of them realized your talents had started coming in. Which you might not have hid as well as you think, but up till then Bell just thought it was you being fourteen."

A grimace; all her quills bristling again, after the distractions of the camp had finally laid them flat. "Why should I care? Why should they? They all thought I was next door to being a murderer."

"They cared. Well, I s'ppose the youngsters were mostly oblivious, but the grownups were near frantic. People are complicated like that. I'd promised to haul you home if I found you." *By the scruff of the neck, if need be,* he'd implied; now, there was an obsolete plan. "If I'm not going to keep that promise...it's going to be tricky to explain why I've taken over as your patrol leader if your Lakewalker blood's to be kept a secret from half the people reading the letter and half not."

A twitch. But she didn't gainsay this.

"Now, I don't think it's a secret that *can* be kept anymore, but I don't feel it's mine to choose. Is it yours?"

Her hands hesitated; resumed braiding. She stared down at her work. "Maybe not," she said at last. And then, "...No."

"Think a little on what we should say, then." The mist was collecting into heavier droplets, drifting downward; time to go inside. She cast one wry glance at him trying to manage his stick and lift the heavy kettle, and forthrightly took it away from him.

LUNCH AND THE drizzle finished at about the same time, so Barr led Lily back across camp to the patrol headquarters, that being the best place to find paper, pens, ink, and the courier schedule. By a stroke of great luck, Amma was out, and her assistant helped him to the supplies with no more than a curious glance. He sat Lily down at the side of the map table and flattened out his cadged paper, gnawing his lip. *Think of it as a patrol report. Short and to-the-point.* He dipped the quill and began to write.

To the Mason family, Tamarack Farm, Hackberry Corner.

I found Lily safe about a day's ride south of Glassforge. I've taken her to Pearl Riffle Camp to rest up at my mother's tent.

Yes, good idea to get mention of Kiska in there. Bell and Iris should both realize what that meant. *You can write back to me as* Barr Foxbrush, Pearl Riffle Camp, *and give it to this courier or any Lakewalker to pass along. It will find us in a while.*

There was a lot of page left, even when he signed it large and clear.

He shoved it around to Lily. "You should add something in your own hand, to show I'm not sending them a tarradiddle."

She took the quill and scowled at the paper, though seemingly more in concentration than anger, because she dipped and began a careful, scratchy print. He watched sidewise as the words and her thinking trickled out.

We ran across a blight bogle on the trail. They are real!!! Barr got hurt but will get better. Barr's brother Bay and some patrollers went to kill it. I'm all right. So is Moon. The camp is interesting. There are a lot of women here doing things. A long pause, and she crouched again. *The river is big.*

After another minute or two spent staring at this desperately neutral recitation of inarguable facts, she gave up and signed her name.

"That will likely do," Barr reassured her. And himself. "It doesn't have to be the last letter ever."

"I wish it was," she muttered.

Unsure how to respond, he let that go by. "Anyway, if there's anything you want to add but not put in writing, you can give the courier a short message to deliver by word of mouth. Of course, then you've got to trust the courier, but they mainly don't care what you tell them. They just pass it on same as the letters. I figure to say, Tell Miz Bluebell Mason, but no one else, *Lily's growing Lakewalker powers.* Four words, one ear, it won't be mixed up. But somebody there needs to know why I haven't just trotted you right back, or they'll be making up tales for themselves." Barr shuddered at the more lurid possibilities. "Ate you and boiled your bones, or worse."

She looked startled. "What's worse?"

He rubbed his face. Did *not* scratch at his stitches. "Never mind. But I'm sure you've heard gossip about patroller necromancers, even if not in your house."

"Well, yeah, but mostly kids' talk, whispers under the blankets. I thought it wasn't really real, same as...blight bogles." She hesitated, contemplating this contradiction.

"I already handed you the heart of us, out on the trail." He touched where the bone knife hilt would be at his waist, if he hadn't laid it aside atop Bay's trunk. "Just as soon as I could. Maybe that was the wrong order, I dunno. But the rest is only filling out the details."

She frowned at his gesture. "Will I get one of those human-bone knives like yours? If they let me stay?"

He flinched, and evaded, "They're for grownups. Children don't share."

"I'm not hardly a child anymore. How old were you?"

"...Sixteen. As soon as I had the range and control to patrol." Not very good control yet, but a young patroller wouldn't get better by sitting in a tent. And how anxiously avid he had been to get bonded to his own sharing knife, proud outward marker of adulthood! He'd barely thought deeper than that, then. What should you call a wise thing done for fool reasons?

Clothes made big for growing into, maybe.

Lily sucked her lip, thinking who-knew-what. Not Barr, unfortunately.

Barr folded and sealed the letter, and handed it in to the right courier bag, together with a note for the courier to see him at Tent Foxbrush before riding out tomorrow morning. Which meant someone would be waking him up at a hideous hour, but it couldn't be helped. Maybe he could hit his bunk early. Was now too early? Verel had been right, blight him. Barr wouldn't have been fit for riding the length of the camp today, let alone the length of the river road. He motioned Lily to follow and limped toward the door.

Only to backstep nearly into her as Captain Osprey blew in.

Amma halted too, looking them over. "There you two are." She sounded...actually, not much more dyspeptic than usual. Anyway, not with that tight, scalding edge of fury leaking between her teeth that Barr could remember from prior incidents.

"Ah. Amma. Hiya." Barr attempted a grin, suspected it made him look like a sick possum, and gave it up. He straightened instead. Backing another half step, he put his arm around Lily's shoulders. "I don't think you met my daughter last night. Miss Lily Mason of Hackberry

Corner. Lily, this is the Pearl Riffle Camp patrol captain, Amma Osprey."

"Yeah, I heard the story about that," said Amma. "From the horse girls. And Verel and Yina. And your grandmother."

She'd have encountered the horse girls when seeing the relief patrol off at dawn. That would likely have sent her back to the medicine tent. Whether she'd cornered the head of Tent Foxbrush, or the other way around, Barr couldn't guess, but the two were near-contemporaries and long-time cronies, so they wouldn't have delayed. It did suggest she was fully caught up already, but then, this was Amma.

"Haven't heard your side yet. Curiously." This dry observation was accompanied by that particular ironic eyebrow twitch that Barr knew and loathed so well.

"Is she your boss?" whispered Lily, leaning up to his ear.

"She's everybody's boss."

The corner of Amma's lip twitched. "And don't you forget it, boy." She closed the door firmly—no escape, blight it—and strode to her desk, herding Barr and perforce Lily before her.

She hitched up one haunch on the corner, eyeing Barr. He stiffened and tightened his arm around Lily, whose ground was growing ever more anxious. *Stop leaking, Barr. It's not fair to burden her with your saddlebags.* He took a breath and eased his grip, letting his arm fall.

"Sitting on this news for fifteen years, I hear tell?" said Amma blandly.

"Twelve. If you want to be exact. I didn't know myself until then. I kept a watch after."

"And what would have become of that little patrol if anything had happened to you?"

"Remo knew. And Dag and Fawn."

"Remo! Huh. Might have guessed that. So you weren't riding bare." Patroller slang for riding without a primed knife; in other words, unprepared. Her eyes grew less threateningly narrow, to Barr's confusion. She...liked that he'd taken care? *Well, and what else but that does Amma do, all day and every day?* The recognition made for an odd shifting in his brain from *Nags young patrollers; dodge!*

"It didn't seem like a good idea to leave no reserve, no," said Barr.

Her gaze swung to the tense Lily, and she frowned and gestured. "Oh, pull over a couple of chairs and sit down."

Barr, still at rigid attention, blinked. "Really?"

"You ain't a youngster any more. When more's expected of you, you get more slack."

Barr tried to work out if that was reassuring or ominous as he followed instructions. Lily perched on the edge of her seat like a bird ready to take flight. Barr grunted as he lowered himself, relieving his still-throbbing leg.

"Yeah, you look about like what Verel said you would today," murmured Amma, taking in the details of his physical state with much the same unflattering attention as she'd turn on a patrol horse that had pulled up lame.

"I was a thousand miles of tired *before* I reached Hackberry Corner," Barr sighed. And then floated the question he'd had no chance to ask anyone yet: "How did the farmer-patroller scheme here fare in my absence?"

"It's still going, I expect you'll be pleased to know. We have the usual mix of volunteers, boys out for a lark who don't last, and serious folks who've lost kin to malice attacks, who do. It dropped a little drive without you to spur it along. Your stint in Luthlia was supposed to raise your clout."

He squeezed one eye shut, then the other, without light dawning. "...And then what?"

She shrugged. "As a patrol leader, you'd have had more muscle to run things your way than as a patroller. Or puppeteer, to hear your poor leaders tell it. I'm not so sure what this does to that plan, when it becomes so clear that your motives were more personal. And some folks called you a farmer-lover *before* this."

Barr straightened, pricked into anger. "Lily has no bearing on that! If you cast your mind back, you might remember that I was proposing mixing for the Pearl Riffle patrol right after I got back from the trip up the Trace, which was even before I found out about her. Remo and I got behind the farmer-patroller scheme and pushed because we thought it was *right*, not because I thought it would serve me specially. Well, any more than it serves everyone alive."

She brushed her finger over her lips and regarded him narrowly. "That so."

"Yes," he growled.

Lily tugged his sleeve and looked at him big-eyed, clearly wondering if she dared interrupt this bracing exchange of views with questions.

Barr eased his tone. "Aye, Lily?"

"What are you talking about?"

Amma folded her arms. "This whole scheme for putting farmers on patrol with maker-made groundshields started with Barr. Well, Barr and his friends Dag and Arkady, who'd worked out the first makings. It's all spread out from Pearl Riffle, since. Not something I ever imagined my camp would be famous for. Or notorious, depending on folks' feelings for the try-out."

"Oh." Lily hesitated. "I didn't know that." She eyed Barr sideways. He shifted uncomfortably. What was that vile Hackberry rumor, that patrollers were making some kind of mind-slaves of their farmer volunteers, the way a blighted malice did? He supposed it would have to be the job of the returning volunteers to put a bung in that nonsense. He couldn't be everywhere.

"I'm a good tent-woman," said Amma, "so I purely hate waste. Which haste makes, they say. Verel says you're on camp rest till those stitches come out. That's when *he* decides they do, not when you get impatient and start picking at them, Barr, he told me to mention for some reason that you would know." She snorted. "So I'm not going to be saying anything one way or another about your future as a patroller till I need to. And I'm Tent Osprey, not Tent Foxbrush, so it's not my place to be telling them how to go on."

Barr considered how tight-braided Amma was with his grandmother, and thought, *Yeah, right.* He rubbed his gritty eyes, in lieu of scratching his neck. "About Lily's place. In the camp, not just my tent."

"Mm?"

"She's trained up to do most of the everyday tasks of a tent-woman already. She could be a horse-girl as she stands."

Lily perked in sudden attention.

"I suspect she could make a patroller when she's older, and *not* just as a shielded farmer-helper. Verel thinks"—Barr swallowed—"she could even be bonded to a sharing knife, in time. Thing is, she's not some helpless tiny orphan. She only has to learn the Lakewalker parts. She could be an asset, to any tent willing to see and think clear."

"But she's not independent yet, neither," observed Amma.

"Who of us is?"

A conceding nod. She was watching him struggle with disturbing shrewdness, Barr thought, and he didn't think she was only timing how long it took him to drown himself. *And Lily,* he was reminded, roped together as they were.

Even as a youngster he'd dimly recognized that Amma'd wanted him to be not so much good, as a good patroller. He saw that more keenly now. She was not his adversary in this, though she was surely his judge. He'd planted the ideas in her head about Lily he wanted to have grow there. *Now, clumsy paws off; wait.*

"Barr," said Amma, swinging off her desk, "you're cluttering up my busy headquarters. Go along and get out from

under my feet, until you are back on yours. Ain't no fun trying to spar with a man who looks like a lump of wet mud."

"Hey! I had a bath at Verel's last night."

"Not what I was talking about, and you know it." Her
sharp gaze could have skinned a deer. "I'll find you when
I'm ready."

Barr didn't need to be told again. He towed Lily out.

Wondering what Amma had been planting right back in
him, all along.

ON THE LIMP back to Tent Foxbrush, Lily asked, "What
happens to orphans around here? And"—her voice caught,
forged on—"and bastards?"

"We don't exactly have either, not the way farmers do. All
children born, no matter who their fathers are, are counted
as members of their mother's tent. Girls forever—they *become*
the tent—boys till they go out and get string-bound."

"What if a woman has all boys?"

"Sometimes, one'll bring in a tent-sister to be heiress."
Sometimes, the tent goes dark.

"What if a tent was wiped out all but one?"

"That wouldn't likely happen except maybe in case of a
bad malice attack, like that one over in Raintree, and even
then, most of the camp got out. Or a fi—flood. In which
case, folks would cut and sew as needs be. No one gets left."
He hesitated. "Yours is a trickier coat to stitch, because you
really don't have a mother's tent. Doesn't mean it can't be

done, nor never has before… Also, I've learned more'n a few things about *never been done before.*"

Lily's face pinched in thought as they stumped along. "Could we be our own tent?"

"With the one dependent on the one out on the trail? Hard to see how to hold up a tent with only two pegs." His brows knotted. "Thing is, everything patrollers need to ride out is made by their kin-tents, from clothes to gear to food to, well, people themselves. And anything the tent can't supply has to be traded for, so the kin also need to make a surplus to sell, like Shirri's honey and candles.

"Also…" He mulled, trying to figure how to say this to her. "I never learned all I learned from just one person, such as, say, my dad." And wasn't that going to be a bracing exchange of views, once Oris Foxbrush returned from patrol. "I learned from everybody around me, tent-kin and camp mates and patrol partners, and, yeah, farmers, and rivermen, and I suppose bandits—those were some sharp lessons—and on and on." *And now from you. Huh.* "For years. It's never stopped." He was beginning to suspect it wasn't going to, and was that bad or good?

Her shoulders hunched. "It's discouragin' hard to start a job when you know it won't ever be finished."

"Welcome to patrolling," he murmured dryly. "You don't finish. You just pass it on."

"Like being a farmwife, I guess." She gave a short nod, as if driving in some new peg to brace the tent of her understanding.

Barr blinked. "Uh…" It took him a minute to see her point, another to reluctantly agree. "Same jobs over and over, all have to be done again tomorrow or something dies? Despite the weather or the hurting, or, or whatever. Yeah, I guess there are some parallels." While he was weighing this, his mouth kept moving without him. "Or maybe it's just called being a grownup." He frowned at the words that had fallen out, but felt no urge to call them back.

"Huh," echoed Lily.

BARR SPENT THE trailing remains of the day puttering around the tent in a sodden sort of haze. That was the trouble with slowing down. It let things catch up with you. Though he dutifully, if sluggishly, applied himself to whatever sit-down task someone bothered to shove into his hands. Lily, he was pleased to see, was let to help out too, each in the series of small tasks deftly done another little chink in the Foxbrush walls. Proud principles were all very well, but they tended to make way when so much work needed to be got through somehow. He suspected that wasn't just a Lakewalker trait.

In the early evening, when he was about to give up and crawl into Bay's bunk, Yina Mink came around to check on her patients. Even Lily was wilting by then, and won a touch of ground reinforcement against any lingering blight burn. Yina made Barr sit up on the sawn-log stool in his bunk room for some more concentrated attention.

"Yes, these are trying to go hot," she remarked, her fingers trailing over the snags of stitches and leaving a coolness in their wake. "You'll need a few more treatments to keep them from suppurating. For your strained leg, tent rest will do."

"Can't you give that a boost, speed things along?"

"Tent rest means *at* your tent, not thumping all over camp, so some built-in hobbles are more help than hindrance." She flashed a Verel-like smirk. "The first thing I was taught as a medicine maker was not to waste my reserves on anything that will get better on its own."

"Mm," he allowed, glumly.

"How are things settling in otherwise? With you and your tent-kin and your surprise farmer girl."

Was she still feeling apologetic for her blunder of last night? She shouldn't, Barr decided. There were worse ways the truth could have come out.

"Better than I'd feared," Barr admitted. Apart from his own embarrassments, which were about what he'd expected and which, it seemed, he was just going to have to eat. "Not yet as well as I hope." He considered. "No one here has insulted Lily for being what she is, thanks be. Though I suppose she's bound to strike some mouthy fool somewhere in camp sometime. I should likely talk to her about that hazard. Shirri's youngsters take her for a novelty, Shirri is too run off her legs to say much, and my grandmother, well, I never could read her. She must have been able to put up a whopping groundshield back in her patroller days. My mother seems mainly worried this'll ruin my chances of getting string-bound." If Kiska brought it up again, he should just say he could clear her tent by riding back to Luthlia, ha, now there was the right place for that bluff. All thousand miles, shuddering gods, talk about an empty threat.

"I don't know," said Yina, moving around behind him to treat his other side. "It could be a benefit. The challenge might simply filter out women who weren't up to your weight."

Barr wasn't just sure how to take that. Yina seemed too grave a woman to be flirting, though he did flick a glance to her left wrist, where no binding braid circled. *Hnh. Why not?*

"Verel said you'd spent some time training upriver?" he asked instead. "With Dag and Arkady?"

"Yes, they're amazing groundsetters, aren't they? The medicine work they're doing on farmers was a revelation to me. Your name was mentioned there, by the way."

With a heroic effort, Barr managed not to ask what had been said, but other gossip about these mutual friends filled the rest of his treatment, and then some. He was feeling pretty heartened by the time Yina took her leave. Clearly, she was good at her work.

OVER THE NEXT few days, as Barr gradually emerged from his fatigue fog and his leg stopped throbbing as much, one of his problems was solved as Raki launched Lily into the mob of her Foxbrush cousins. There were at the moment about five of the cubs, including Raki and her next brother Azio, close enough in age to move as their own little patrol. Raki was the natural ringleader, a position unthreatened by the somewhat older Lily due to her off-balance diffidence from being thrust into this strange new world. Lily might seem more prize or pet or patrol souvenir to Raki than tent-sister, so far, but it occurred to Barr, watching them all thump by, that he needn't start only at the top on his scheme of easing Lily into his tent. As a Foxbrush possession, if not yet member, Lily fell naturally within a certain boundary of protection.

He'd run with a similar posse at about that age, he recalled, most from neighboring tents as he'd been a little too young to trail after his siblings, the eldest of whom had already passed into the sphere of the grownups. Some were friends still, like Remo. The adults in this realm had existed mostly as taken-for-granted furniture, to be routed around as the evasion of chores was refined to a skill, and the finding of trouble to an art form. He wondered now if all the crap they'd got away with was due to their own luck, or just the fact that the grownups were too blighted busy or tired to ride them down.

The first expected incident of insult for Lily's farmer-ness was relayed to him, indignantly, not from Lily but from Raki.

"He called her a farmer bastard!" complained Raki. "I kicked him in the knee, and we tried to push him into the river, but he ran away."

Having ascertained that the miscreant was eleven, and not some unpleasant grownup, Barr mentally excused himself from the duty of tracking him down and vigorously adjusting his thinking. He tried not to feel too thankful.

Lily, listening to this field report more in embarrassment than outrage, made a motion of denial. "It wasn't that big a deal. I am, aren't I? It wasn't not *true*."

Ah. Yes. Being bitten by a squirrel might not seem like such an important injury when you were still recovering from being gutted by a bear. *Words won't break bones* seemed like the lying-est lie Barr had ever been told, as a child. Bones knit eventually, he knew from close personal experience. The scars of slander, an insult not just delivered but *believed*, might never heal in a lifetime. Best you could do was bury the stitches under a load of fresh experiences, drop in so much new there was no time left to brood over the old.

And then he wondered if he was accidentally doing something very right for Lily, after all.

LILY'S REPEATED VISITS to Moon, at the patrol paddocks, also slid naturally into acceptance among the horse-girls. Because who among them would turn down a volunteer that regarded currying out mud from coats, combing manes, picking hooves, and mucking stalls as just as high a treat as they did? Lily spent more and more hours over there, and Barr, after observing a few times from a careful distance, left her to it. When she returned, happily reeking of horse—an aroma to which no one in Tent Foxbrush had objections—and checked in with Barr, her confident tales told finally began to outnumber her anxious questions asked.

And so, in this hesitant balance, five days slid by. Barr was keeping count.

Looking up from that afternoon's chore of tending the whole roasting pig that the tent had gone together on, Barr was still taken aback when he saw Lily trooping home from the direction of the paddocks flanked by Bay on one side and Oris Foxbrush on the other. Oris was another sturdy-built Foxbrush of middle height, braided blond hair barely silvering; Tent Grayjay by birth, but looks blending in so well some joked Kiska had picked him like matching a wagon horse.

From her gestures, Lily was retelling the tale of Barr versus the mud-man. Both men were listening closely, Bay smirking, Oris with a sort of bemused professional interest. Clearly, Bay's foray against the sessile must have concluded successfully, and their father's more routine patrol likewise. As patrol leader, Oris would have reported in first to Amma. And received a report in return, *urgh*. Something blunt and forceful, no doubt, but, Barr conceded, honest—as Amma saw things.

How Oris saw things, well, Barr was about to find out. He felt a fresh pang for the forfeited goal of Clearcreek.

The homecoming was expected, hence the pig. But Barr hadn't imagined both patrols arriving atop each other, nor his father meeting Lily before he could explain. All the careful introductions he'd mentally rehearsed were knocked from their saddle. He'd have to scramble to catch a trailing rein.

Lily was casting wary, fascinated glances up at this unexpected grandfather, and Barr realized he didn't actually know what *grandfather* had meant to her at Hackberry Corner. Oris was being polite back at her, near as Barr could tell with the man's ground almost closed. Bay walked half-disregarded at her other elbow, not as an assumed support but perhaps as a known non-threat, and wasn't that interesting.

Barr waved a welcome as they all ambled up to the smoking fire pit; Bay sniffed in hungry appreciation. His glance at Barr was oddly reflective, but a first malice kill would do that to a fellow, even one more of a pest than his middle brother. Barr was reminded that there was more than one homecoming here as his father stepped back and looked him up and down.

"Well. You made it back in one piece after all. There were side bets, you know."

"Did you win or lose?"

Oris grinned. "Not telling you."

But they both dropped their groundshielding briefly, which for a Lakewalker might be as good as a hug. Oris surveyed Barr with that swift patrol-leader summation; what he made of it, Barr couldn't tell, but if he'd been a horse he thought he might have been approved for saddling up. Oris's glance caught briefly on the stitches still embroidering his neck, and his grin dropped to grimace, tilting. "Still up to your old tricks, I see."

"It's...not my fault?"

Oris puffed a laugh. "So I heard tell." He jerked his head toward Lily, who'd been drawn into a discussion of their impending supper by Bay, and lowered his voice. "And that?"

"That one's all mine," Barr sighed.

"*Baarrrr...*"

That familiar intonation dragged like a rake over his nerves. *Don't you start.* He growled under his breath, "I've had the lecture from Remo, Dag, Fawn, mother, grand-mother, Shirri, and Amma. So far. Not to mention what all Bluebell had to say." Still fiercely painful in his mem-ories, old and more recent. "D'you really think it needs repeated?"

"Don't know. Did you ever do it again?"

"No!"

"Then I guess not."

Silence. Barr gaped a little. "That's it?"

Oris's eyebrows went up. "You want more? I could oblige you, but I'm tired."

"No, not...yeah, that's fine, more than fine, but I mean, about Lily."

He followed Barr's gaze to his surprise granddaugh-ter. Pursed his lips. Murmured, "I believe that wants some thinking before talking. We'll take her up later."

I just had to ask... And then, more soberly: *Yeah. I did. I do.*

Oris turned away into the oncoming rush of the Foxbrush women and children who had spotted his arrival and pelted from the tent, variously shrieking, yelling welcome, grin-ning, or just smirking in satisfaction depending on their ages. From Kiska, Oris got an actual hug. Lily stepped back a few paces and watched this with guarded, flicking eyes, maybe trying to sort out who meant what to each other. Observant, apart. Lonely in a crowd?

Barr stepped over to her and tried the shoulder-hug, which only got brushed off with a halfhearted prickle.

"I'm all right," she muttered. "It's just a lot."

"I 'spect so."

"Though you should've seen the patrol paddocks, with sixty horses coming in at once." She brightened. "It was an uproar like a, a, I don't know what. Nothing I ever seen."

Barr had, often enough in the past. Maybe a different mood when patrols were bringing in injured or dead or other bad news, or a new primed knife, a gift everyone and no one wanted. But they seemed to have escaped all that today; good. "Exciting?"

"I guess! And all those patrollers making noise. I thought you people were *quiet*."

"When running a pattern-sweep, sure. Silent as death. When we finally get done with duty someplace safe, the lid comes off. Pretty rowdy, were they?"

"The ones from Bay's patrol were. The ones from your father's patrol seemed kind of envious, by the way they were razzing the others." She reflected. "They insulted each other something fierce, but nobody got mad. They were mainly laughing."

"Patroller humor. You learn to read it… Ah, don't try out any of that yourself until you know a lot more. There's rules."

"I… 'spect so," she echoed dubiously.

The reunion broke up in the assignment of chores for the impending all-Foxbrush picnic. After an anxious test of the doneness of the pig, Barr and Lily won the task of laying a big basketful of winter-wrinkled yams into the coals to bake. It was too early for strawberries, but there would be a few spring greens, and a big kettle of Shirri's rhubarb cooked with honey, the dried fruits and plunkin strips everyone was tired of, and some real bread made with wheat flour. Yams for all and then some. Food could get a trifle odd when winter's dearth lingered into the first deceptive warmth of spring, but Tent Foxbrush knew how to make do.

The pig, finally uncovered, drew a drooling audience like a gathering of wolves, if wolves came complete with their own offerings of foodstuffs. For a while, all was chaos not unlike, Barr imagined, the recent scene at the patrol paddocks. Near forty Foxbrushes at last sorted themselves out on blankets and logs, and fed each other with enthusiasm. Tales were exchanged like sustenance.

Most of his relatives had pressed Barr's Luthlia stories out of him in bits over the past five days, so he was content to sit back and let Bay, elation badly concealed under a veneer of nonchalance, go on about his first malice kill. Lily seemed quite riveted by his word-picture of 'their' malice's final fate. Whether instigating or trying to be helpful, Bay then drew Lily up to tell her tale of the finding. Only her repeated practice allowed her to stand up to this larger audience, Barr thought; if not with the enthusiasm of

Bay's bragging, at least not as if she were facing a hanging, quite. But she scuttled out of the firelight in a hurry at her first chance.

To Barr's side, he was vaguely warmed to note. He offered her more shreds of pork. "You did good."

"They were laughing at your part," she growled. "I didn't think it was funny. I'd never been more scared in my life." A glum pause. "Except for the fire."

"What you did to that mud-man...rescued the funny so's we could have it now. It's not a bad thing."

She hunched, chewing. "Hm."

ALL THE CLEANUP took them through the sunset, so it was well after dark that Barr found himself finally alone with his father, sitting on upended logs and watching the last of the embers burn out in the big firepit. The blessed lack of an opinionated audience favored what Barr wanted to accomplish, and he wondered if that feeling was reciprocated. Neither of them seemed in a hurry to start. A younger Barr might have jibed and jabbed, coaxing lumps just to get it over with. Now he was content to wait.

"So," said Oris, and leaned forward with a stick to poke a few last orange sparks skyward. "You've known about this girl for fifteen years?"

"Twelve, but yeah, more or less. I first found out about her the winter after Remo and I got back from that trip to the Graymouth. She was rising two, then."

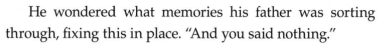

He wondered what memories his father was sorting through, fixing this in place. "And you said nothing."

"Was I wrong? Then?"

A shrug. "Twelve years ago, maybe not. It might have been the last straw in a whole big heap you'd piled up, and I was already hankering to set your hair on fire. You had such a talent for making me furious. Amma, too. She could never decide whether to be furious along with me, or blame me for your existence, so she did both. Still more so, right after you and Remo broke his great-grandmother Grayjay's primed knife and fled down the river."

That had been a conflagration already in progress, Barr thought. It had hardly needed more fuel. "Strictly speaking, Remo fled. Amma sent me after him. And I did bring him back—eventually—so, patrol accomplished." The coals glowed dully in the dark, tamed by time to use, not hazard. "And a whole lot of other things along-with, that I'd never have learned otherwise."

"That I did observe. Even back then. Watching you work up your farmer-patroller scheme, after, you surprised me with your sticking-to. It hasn't gone near as bad since then as I'd feared it might, either. Still a lot to be proved, mind."

His father had been one senior patroller whose, if not support, at least lack of opposition had allowed Barr to push the idea into tentative reality, all those years ago. And he'd accepted groundshielded farmer apprentices into his own patrol, teaching them right along with the camp youngsters. Barr owed him a lot for that.

"At least we're getting a chance to prove it. Not just argue about it, around in useless circles."

Oris nodded in a conceding sort of way. After a few minutes, while the firepit's heat grew fainter against their faces, he went on, "Been thinking this about your Lily. If I, or you, or any other patroller, were to encounter some lost orphan on the road with Lakewalker powers, it'd be our clear duty to bring that child into camp for taking care of. Some camp, somehow. I'm trying to work out the ways this is different, with her parentage being known, and not really seeing... Well, there might be special complications. Amma said you two'd written a letter to her farm?"

"Yes. There's hardly been time for anyone to write back, though."

"I can see a half-a-dozen troubles might come of that for the tent, or the camp. From awkward to ugly."

"So can I," Barr sighed. "But I can't guess which one to brace for at this range. I tried to keep the letter simple, but I figured it had to go out as soon as might be, to relieve folks' minds of the main worry for her safety. After that, maybe they can think less frantic. I did send a word-of-mouth to Bluebell to let her know about Lily's powers, which was bound to make her mull. I'm hoping any reply will give me some hint what to say better. And more time to think it through."

"You expect a letter? Not her mama showing up at the camp gate to demand Lily back?"

"No, not Bluebell." Of that, Barr was tolerably certain, though he noticed Oris's Lakewalker assumption about which parent was the tent-head. "Even leaving aside how tangled her feelings are about Lily, she's four months pregnant and has a toddler and two other youngsters nailing her feet to the farmhouse floor. And poor Fid was still recovering from his burns. A letter'll be tricky enough to deal with." Much would depend on whether it was addressed to Barr or Lily, or both, and which Mason wrote it, and what they knew and what they wanted, and how Lily reacted, and, and, too many other flailing loose ends, too many of which were not Barr's to tie.

"Hm. At least it's good you're thinking about it. Nothing more to be done about it right now, I guess."

Barr let this undisputable remark sit for a time, as the cool damp of the evening rose from the river, and the first frogs of the season peeped in the distance. Muted voices and an infant's indignant wail sounded from the nearby tents, and someone out on the water, calling. The mutter of the riffle, always on the edge of hearing, filled in.

"So," Barr said at last. "You'll not be pushing to throw both me and Lily out of the tent on our ears?"

"You think you two come as a pair, now?"

"Just like boots," Barr affirmed.

Oris took in this declaration, seeming to digest it for a while. "Well, you know, it's your grandmother Foxbrush who has the final word. Not me."

"Not an answer. I can ask *her* myself. I asked you."

A conceding head-tilt. "Then, I'm not opposin' you."

Slithering in. Smooth enough for going on with. "Thank you."

"So formal, boy!"

Barr shrugged to conceal his relief. "I wasn't looking forward to being forced to choose my child over my parents."

"And would you have?"

"Yes." And was startled at his lack of hesitation.

Oris tossed his stick onto the coals and hoisted himself up to go inside, smiling a bit bleakly. "Well, if so…you'd be doin' it right. I don't know where you learned that from, but I'm glad you did."

Barr sat a moment, getting over the unexpectedness of the exchange. But he did raise his voice to call, as Oris lifted the tent flap, "I hope you like porcupines!"

A pause in the shadows, then a short, fathoming laugh. "I promise I'll take care how I touch her."

FIVE DAYS AFTER the pig picnic, Barr strolled, not hobbled, over to the medicine tent to return his stick and get his stitches taken out. By Verel himself, officially. It did mean he had to sit down in the front room and endure being basted with Verel's stinging spirits, as the threads were clipped and, *ow*, pulled one by one.

"Not bad," said Verel judiciously. "The scars are still going to be tender and swollen for a little while, but they didn't blow up into a roaring infection after all."

"They tried, for a bit." Giving Barr a feverish headache for a couple of days. "Yina's reinforcements pushed that back pretty good. She took care of the adhesions that were grabbing hold, too." He twisted his neck to demonstrate the lack of internal tugging, and Verel *tch'd* and tapped his chin to still him. "She looks to be coming on for a strong maker."

"Yes, she's my best apprentice in quite a while. She could start working on her own any time, back at Log Hollow. I wish I could devise some way to keep her here at Pearl Riffle."

"I, ah...noticed she doesn't seem to be string-bound. Does she have a fellow here?"

Verel snickered. "She has fellows here following her around like a herd of moonstruck foals. She didn't tell you all about Rett, back at Log Hollow?"

"No?"

"Huh." Verel pulled another stitch.

"Who's Rett?"

"A right paragon of a young man, to hear her tell it. He does everything better than anyone, and is waiting for her faithfully. Writes to her regular. There might be poems."

"Oh," said Barr, slumping on the stool.

"Sit up." Clip, tug.

"Mph."

"But she didn't tell you?"

"Not a word. Although I can't say as I asked. She was always in a hurry, and there was Lily to check, too."

Verel grinned. The expression was disturbingly sneaky. "That's interesting."

Barr was reminded of his feelings about that term in medicine makers' mouths.

Verel went on, "Because she tells *everyone* about Rett. Yet not you."

"So?"

Verel leaned over and flicked him on the forehead with a strong, albeit clean, fingernail.

"Ow! Stop *doing* that, Verel!" Barr batted at his hand, careful not to actually connect. "What riddle d'you think I'm supposed to be solving now, with no blighted information as usual?"

"Rett is a tarradiddle. Yina didn't want distractions in her studies, so she made him up. She's very determined."

"Oh." Barr blinked. "...Really?"

"She's worked out his whole life story. I make suggestions to add, now and then. It's been fairly entertaining."

"And no one's guessed?"

"She has patroller-grade groundshielding. And can be very straight-faced." Verel smirked.

"Unlike you... And how was I supposed to figure that out?"

"It could be a test."

Barr scowled, or tried to. His lips kept tugging up. "Then why are you helping me cheat?"

"Maybe because some things are just too painful to watch? I mean, despite the amusement."

"Proud to serve," Barr growled. But, after a moment, "So, uh...has Yina said anything about me?"

"That would be telling." Clip, tug. "Well, she's reported on your recovery, and Miss Lily. But I haven't heard much news about Rett lately. Poor fellow. I suspect he's fated for a sad end."

"A fatal accident?" Barr could come up with some suggestions. *Tarradiddles, heh.*

"Mm, I'd vote for a last heartbreaking letter telling her how he's tired of waiting and has found someone else, and is moving after her to another hinterland. Much tidier."

"I can see that." A last clip. "Thanks, Verel."

"The rest is up to you, mind." Tug. "Don't muck this one up. I'd be peeved."

"There's not a rush, I guess. Is there?"

"She wasn't planning to return to Log Hollow for a couple more months, no."

"Is she tent-heiress there for the Minks?"

"Nope. Younger sister. Of four. So somewhat detachable, I'd gauge. If she had a strong enough reason."

Younger sisters were known to move out and start their own tents, time to time, if things grew too crowded and tense. Like young queen bees. Conditions had to be just right, though. *Hmm.*

Verel turned away to tidy up, and said over his shoulder, "So how is your Miss Lily doing, down among all the Foxbrushes?"

"Not…badly. She's a lot calmer than when we first arrived. I was afraid I might have to fight to defend her, which would have set folks' backs up something fierce. But really, it seems to be working better to just let things slide quietly along until the question is settled without anyone, y'know, actually settling it." Barr mulled how to sum this up. "She's learning a lot very fast, and most of it isn't even coming from me. Raki's taken her all around the camp. The horse-girls have been showing her how they use groundsense tricks to control the horses, and practicing shielding, because a lot of them are just learning that skill themselves. All the tent chores aren't too much different from what she did back on the farm, apart from some groundwork flourishes added. She has a temper, but the occasional knock she encounters for being farmer doesn't seem to kick it up. I'm not sure why that is."

"She doesn't know it's supposed to be an insult?"

"Maybe... No, I don't think it's that." Barr's lips twisted. "I can't tell if it's because she expects not to have her feelings considered, or she doesn't feel secure enough to hit back. Or if she just brushes off crap from fools. Which would be pretty mature for her age."

"Or any age," agreed Verel.

Barr touched his fingers gingerly to his dotting of new scabs; Verel, with a mild sigh, knocked his hand away.

"So am I cleared to go back to patrol?" Barr had uncomfortably mixed feelings about that. He'd been looking forward to reestablishing himself at Pearl Riffle, but then things had got...complicated. Lily still seemed like a fresh-transplanted seedling, raw and torn, with no roots put down yet enough to hold her in a high wind. Who would look to watering her every day if he were gone from the tent? So to speak. He imagined her irate response to such a comparison, and pressed out a grin.

"At need. The rest will be up to Amma, now."

"Isn't it always."

TWO DAYS AFTER that, a young messenger from patrol head-quarters ran Barr to earth at Tent Foxbrush, where he was sitting out front in the sunlight mending riding leathers, to breathlessly announce he was to report at once to Amma, along with Miss Lily.

Barr set down the awl. "Is it an emergency?" A call-up for a reserve patrol should not have included Lily. His glance around saw no signs of a sudden rise in the river, flash flood-ing from unseen rains far upstream needing all available hands to help at the ferry. No smoke billowed up from any-where across the camp marking some out-of-control fire.

The youth shook his head. "I don't think so. But she did say not to dawdle."

"Did she, now?"

The runner smirked. "Well, she actually said to tell him to hustle his dragging tail, and bring his other tail, too."

"Close enough." Barr waved acknowledgment, and the runner trotted off to deliver his next message wherever.

Barr detoured to the patrol paddocks to pick up Lily. The stables were quiet, confirming no patrol crisis in progress. He found her having a commune with Moon, lying atop his bare back as he nibbled his way peacefully around the pasture. She slid off and bounced over to Barr at his beckoning wave.

"What is it?"

"Amma wants to see the pair of us."

"Oh? Why?"

"Runner didn't say."

They trudged southwest along the valley's slope, head-quarters-ward. The noon air was hazily bright, soft with the familiar smell of the river. Barr went on cautiously, "Now, I know Amma can be pretty, uh, blunt, but don't let her scare you. She generally only gets a bur under her saddle if it's something important." Or if a fellow had irritated her one time too many, but they'd hardly spoken in the past few days.

"I didn't think she was all that scary. I like her."

"Angry Amma?" said Barr, startled. "Whyever?"

Lily frowned and shrugged, plainly trying to piece together some new idea. "Thing is…she may get mad, but she isn't whiny or naggy about it. She doesn't store it up like a, a compost heap, all hot on the inside and rotting. She's angry like she has a *right*, and no one disputes it." She added after a moment, "Or tells her to be a good girl, or be quiet, or apologize. Or go to her room."

Barr's brain sagged, trying to imagine anyone trying any such thing on Amma. She must have been fourteen once, too, but he found he could only picture young Amma as a sawed-off version of her current self, complete with the gray braid and the gift for sarcasm. He shook his head to clear the image.

"I like the way she's angry," Lily concluded, in a tone of bemused discovery. "It's just all out there in front of you, not lying up hidden to ambush you later."

It was a view of Amma he'd never considered. "You have a point, Porcupine."

She made a wry face at the nickname, which looked to be here to stay. Like the girl herself, he trusted. "If I really am a porcupine, I ought to have a lot of them."

Barr's lips twitched up. "Could be." A belated question occurred to him. "So when have you seen Amma enough to talk to?"

"Oh, she comes around to the paddocks pretty often, to check on the horses and gear, and tell people what's going to need doing. And figure out what she can count on to do it with. She lets me help her with some things."

"Ah." All right, he'd hoped Lily would find lots of other Pearl Riffle folks to model her new self on, but *Amma?* That was mildly terrifying.

…It made him grin.

The headquarters building hove into view, quiet on this peaceful day. Two mounts were tied to the hitching rail out front, a horse and a pony; not tacked up like courier horses. Not Lakewalker at all. All his fretting about how to answer the next letter from Hackberry was wasted, it seemed. Barr recognized that pony.

So did Lily. She breathed an odd little *Oh,* and her steps faltered. He could feel her senses extend, then snap half-closed in the tightest shielding she'd yet achieved, but there was no time to praise her.

"Chin up," he murmured. "You've seen a malice; nothing else can ever be as bad."

She shot him a vexed look. "It's not the same thing."

Nor the same kind of courage needed? Maybe so. He reflected on his own earlier attempt to avoid Pearl Riffle and Tent Foxbrush, and how much he'd rather have had a malice. Of course, with his luck, he'd got both.

He opened the door for her and entered on her heels, his own deep sense reaching out into the dimmer interior while sight caught up.

Only four people present: Amma perched on her desk edge; her assistant Ryla, who was fussing about the hob with a kettle for tea; Fiddler Mason and his son Reeve, parked on stools facing Amma. All looked up as they entered.

Fid was still bandaged to the elbows, extra wrappings around his hands to protect them from the road dirt. The swathing seemed mostly for guarding the tender new scars from knocks, the bulk of the burns beneath near-healed, though a nasty suppuration troubled his right hand where the damage had dug deepest. He looked tired and strained.

Reeve had collected even more road dirt since whenever they'd started out from Hackberry Corner, although on a twelve-year-old it looked natural. He seemed tense, mistrustful, peeved. Right; Fid couldn't have taken to the trail in his condition without a helper, and so his eldest son had presumably been conscripted. They seemed to be the only Masons in the delegation.

Fid rose as the door shut behind them. "Lily! You are here!"

Lily stopped short. "We sent the letter saying so." She swallowed. "You must have got it. Why are you here?"

Fid blinked, one swathed hand going out. "To bring you home."

"Oh." It was the most uninviting syllable Barr had ever heard fall from a person's lips, but her ground was in a roil of confusion, belying her still, set face.

"Why didn't you come on your own?" demanded Reeve. "Since you aren't dead in a ditch or anything after all." He frowned at his sister as if her obviously uninjured state were a lapse on her part.

"I *left.* I'd think even you could make that out."

"Well, you didn't leave a note or anything, so how's anyone s'pposed to know where you were going? Everybody was fussed something fierce."

"I'd have figured they'd be relieved."

"Yeah, they weren't." And that water had flowed downhill unfairly, Reeve apparently felt.

Fid made a weary, practiced motion of quashing toward his son. "Pipe down, Reeve." His eyes searched Lily anxiously. "Lily, are you *all right?*" There was a world of dark under-meaning in that inflection which Barr wasn't quite sure Lily got. Which was its own answer, he supposed.

"I said so in our letter. Barr 'n I sat right there"—she pointed to the map table—"and wrote it out together."

It was unhappily apparent that Bell had not yet done the hard work of straightening out Lily's secrets with Fid. *Hoo boy.* Why Bell had let her husband take to the road still unknowing Barr couldn't imagine. Maybe it had been a hot argument. Maybe it had been cold despair. Maybe it had been slithering-out, handing off the problem to Barr as a long-delayed slap.

Didn't matter, Barr decided. It was here, and in his lap, and of all the people he had to take due care for in this, just one came first, jittering stiffly at his side.

Amma was watching all this with her arms tight-crossed. Barr hoped she hadn't scared Fid too much, though he seemed little worse than normally wary for a farmer venturing uninvited into a patroller enclave. Absent gods, what all had she and Fid said to each other while the runner fetched Barr and Lily? Barr's gaze flicked to her face, searching for a sign. Her ground was mostly closed, so no clue there. Though the *You have dumped a mess on my desk and I'm not happy, Barr, and I'm about to share* posture was all too readable.

There was no help for it; he asked her outright. "What all have folks told each other? So far?"

Amma rubbed one bony knuckle across her lips. "Not much, 'cept that Lily was here safe and I'd fetch her out. And you."

Fid turned to Barr, and added earnestly, "And I'm behindhand, Patroller, for thanking you for finding Lily. It wasn't anything you had to go out of your way to do for us, and I'm grateful as I can be."

"Ah, hm. Well." *Ouch.* "Turns out there are some complications about that." A quick glance at Amma, like a drowning man pleading for rescue, found no rope in sight.

Amma inhaled through her nose. "This one's all yours, Barr. I can't sit down and do your talking for you, though it's plain it's time." She jerked her head to the map table, where Ryla was setting out mugs, and conceded, "You can use my table, though."

Not sending them back to the overpopulated Foxbrush den to have the conversation, at least. Barr wasn't sure if his own relatives would hold him out on tongs, or try to mix in, and he didn't want to find out the hard way. He glanced at the rigid Lily; there was far too much at stake here to risk, as Verel put it, mucking this one up. He had never felt more ham-handed.

"Now we've got her, can't we just *leave?*" whined Reeve. "Where's Moon? If Lily's here, that dumb horse has got to be around somewhere."

"Aye," said Fid, "now we've found her safe, we shouldn't bother your camp with our troubles any further, Captain Osprey. I'm very grateful to you for sheltering her. But Lily, it's time to collect your things."

She glanced at Barr. "No," she said slowly, "I don't think it is."

"*Lil-ee,*" said Reeve. "Come *on*. You've put Papa through enough trouble."

Amma cut across Lily's opening mouth. "Ryla, take young master Reeve here and lead their mounts down to the paddocks, let him water them and give them a rub-down, maybe some hay. Take your time."

All right, one rope, but it was shrewdly thrown.

Fid's eyes pinched, as he began to pick up the sense of something not right. He was not by any measure a stupid man, Barr was reminded.

"Yes, do that, Reeve," Fid endorsed this, in a firm paternal tone that Barr envied. "They've carried us a long way, and they've still got to carry us back. And your poor pony's legs had to move twice as much."

"Aww…" But Reeve, at a reinforcing frown from his papa, allowed himself to be herded out. Despite the boy's bellyaching, Barr imagined he must harbor at least some curiosity about his first visit to a Lakewalker camp.

Amma gestured to the table. "Carry on, Barr." She moved around and sat behind her desk to upend a courier pouch and start sorting through its contents. Declining to be run out of her own headquarters for this? Silently backing Barr up? Determined to witness the drama first-hand? She opened the first letter and began to read, neatly managing to be there and not-there simultaneously. Pure smokescreen; she'd be listening to and judging his every word, he had no doubt.

Barr sighed and hauled another chair to the map table. He sorted mugs, putting Fid across the short side from himself, letting Lily pick her own position. She settled herself on the end between them.

While Barr was still scratching how to start, Fid said, "So what's this all about, Mister Patroller?"

So many things. "Ah…did you ever suspect Lily might have Lakewalker blood? Lakewalker powers?" Not hinting how, yet.

Fid leaned back, lips parting, eyebrows going up. "No." A hesitation. "Does she?" His tone was suddenly guarded. But…not shocked.

Hnh. Barr paused, trying to sort out what to say in the face of that.

Lily folded her arms in a rather Amma-like gesture. "I do, Papa. It seems they've been coming on for half a year now, but I didn't know what to make of it. It was just strange and crazy-like, and scary. And then I met Barr, who has them too, and he did know. And a whole lot of things I could never figure out...got figured out." Her lips pressed closed.

Fid cast her a cautious glance. "Did they."

A short silence, while nobody went first. Barr's neck prickled with the conviction that whatever Fid was choosing to conceal, it wasn't going to make anything easier.

Lily blew air through her pursed lips, somewhere between a sigh and a frustrated hiss. And took the bit in her teeth. "Did you always know you weren't my pa—father?"

She was starting to be able to read grounds too, Barr was reminded. Still working out what meaning the sensations conveyed, like a shifting light not seen but felt, mostly intuitive but partly learned. But Fid's ground had to be among the most familiar to her.

Fid's jaw set against some too-sudden reply. She had all his attention, now. Finally, cornered by her unwavering blue gaze, he settled on no-help-for-it simple. "Yes, I did. Couldn't not know, really." He flicked a male-sharing glance at Barr, *I can count to nine,* that tried to leave out Lily.

Which didn't exactly work. Her face bunched in perplexity. "But you married Mama anyway?"

"'Course I did. Some fool had himself a beautiful girl like Bell, and was stupid enough to *throw her away?* I may be some kinds of fool myself, but I was never fool enough for *that*." He huffed out a scornful breath.

Lily unlocked her hand from her mouth to say, "Didn't… Mama know you knew?"

Fid flinched uneasily. "It wasn't something I was going to bring up in the beginning. I just wanted her to be happy, and stay with me. And then, as time went on, it mattered less and less."

"Except now it does," said Lily slowly. "On account of… these things in me."

He frowned at her, but thoughtful, not displeased. Maybe relieved to have the burden of his secret lifted with so startlingly few conniptions? "Yeah, seems so. Lakewalker, huh, can't say as I ever guessed that, though. I suppose it must have been some passing lout of a patroller. I didn't think it could be anyone I knew in Hackberry Corner."

Barr glanced aside to catch Amma eyeing him over her paper. He would rather have jumped into the Riffle while the ice was breaking up, but he could spot the opening as well as she could. Blight it.

Weakly, he raised his hand and waved his fingers. "Lout of a patroller. Ah, that would be me, happens. In my defense, I was only eighteen."

That did get the first shocked rise out of the dauntingly level Fid. "You!" His eyes narrowed abruptly. Beneath the table edge, Barr thought his fists clenched.

"Were you really riding past my brother-in-law's farm on happenstance?"

Absent gods, Barr trusted he wasn't imagining the affair had continued, because that sure wasn't another cut anyone needed to deal Bell. Let him dismiss the notion swiftly, if so... Which he seemed to be doing, judging by the easing from the tight twinge in his ground as he reviewed whatever memories of his marriage overrode it. Sensible man; what had anyone done to deserve him?

And then Barr's heart broke a little more for Lily, and the smear of suspicion that had driven her out onto her lonely road. Blight, but he was beginning to hate this whole snarled cat's cradle of secrets and lies they all seemed to be caught in.

"Ah, no," he put in hastily. "But I only kept a watch on Lily, once I found out about her, which didn't actually happen till she was two. In case just this chance of her throwing Lakewalker might arise, except I was up freezing my tail in Luthlia when the moment came by, and missed it till I was riding home." He hesitated. "I've no idea how things would have gone if I'd spotted it earlier. I don't guess there's any way this could have come out easy. For anyone involved."

A much longer silence, while each digested their separate stock of new revelations.

"I'm afraid your kindness kind of back-blew on Bell, Fid," Barr offered at last. "It gave her a secret she was scared spitless of spilling, to this day. When you get home"—soon, by preference, and he hoped Fid was taking the hint—"you

might want to straighten that out with her, give her ease."
Bell's part of this knot was not Barr's to unravel, but it
appeared Fid had not been entirely blameless after all. It
wasn't culpability, certainly, but perhaps poor judgment—
not from not caring, but from caring too much. *Yeah, there's
a lot of that going around.*

"Mama hated me," Lily muttered, as if determined to
get this out. "I figured that was why."

"No, she doesn't!" said Fid, taken aback. "Sure, you two
fratch some, but families do."

Lily scowled back at him in tight-lipped denial. Barr
didn't think they were going to see eye-to-eye on this one for
maybe another decade. Or two. Or after Lily had children of
her own. Or wait, no, that would make Barr a *grandfather...*

"If it's about Edjer," Fid sighed, "that's just going to take
some getting-over time. It can't be helped." And Barr was
reminded that Fid, too, had buried a boy, and still grieved.

"Barr," said Lily, and suddenly her ground was aflame,
like last night's embers flaring up at a sudden whistling
draft, *"believes* me that I didn't let that fire start, still less set
it a'purpose."

"Does he?" Fid's glance across at Barr grew suddenly keen.
"Do you guess, or do you know? Some Lakewalker magic?"

"Lakewalker magic," Barr decided to simplify this.
"Reading grounds, we call it. We can usually tell if someone is telling the truth or lying, or at least believes they are.
Honestly mistaken being another problem, but that's just as
true for farmers."

Fid sat back, briefly diverted. "Doesn't that get, er, awkward, sometimes?"

"We have some work-arounds, if need drives." *And thanks be for groundshielding.*

A snort from the desk, which Barr ignored. Amma hadn't mixed in so far; Barr wasn't sure if it was because she thought he was doing all right, or she was just letting him hang himself with that rescue-rope.

Fid clasped his hands on the table and stared down at them for a long moment. He finally looked up at Lily: "I did think the odds were in favor of your tale, but I was never sure, you know, one way or another, with how certain Edjer was carryin' on. Didn't see how we ever could be. So we just had to go on somehow."

She stared back, all her old hurts bleeding in her eyes. "And now you still can't be sure," she realized. Her voice was dead level, despair stifled behind set teeth. "Because you can't know if you trust this Lakewalker fellow, either. It doesn't ever get better, does it? It just gets more, one level down."

Barr bit back his belief that once word got out around Hackberry of Lily's Lakewalker blood, there would be a whole new raft of slanderous gossip floated about how she could have started that fire. She didn't need to deal with that crap today, though, so neither did he. At least she didn't seem to be clutching any false optimism. At *fourteen*, gah.

Fid gave up, or let go of something. Of hope, of Lily, of any expectation about how things would be? "Lily, I am so sorry." Not specifying for what, though it was certainly a true statement.

Lily leaned her head back in her chair and rubbed her eyes as if they ached. Or maybe it was her heart. Her lips moved to form some response, but then just blew out her breath in bleak frustration.

"It's time, I think, to close this court," said Barr. "Except… Lily, if you have anything more to say, it's now or never. Because, see, ground reading goes deeper than a person sometimes wants." To that cold little lump of guilt he'd spotted on their first meeting, hidden like a stone in the porridge. Waiting to break teeth. Something about the night of the fire, yet not the fire, it didn't take too many brains to guess. *Fortunately for me.* "Everybody else at this table's taken their turn being rolled in the barrel. It's only fair. If it's making you sick, you need to barf it up." Was that too blunt? But, curse it, if he was being put to shovel out this stable, he was blighted going to finish the job. Because he sure wasn't up for doing it *over.*

A jerk, a startled-deer look. *How did you know? What do you know?* It hardly took groundsense to read that. Briefly, she sat rigid, stiff, resisting.

And broke, thank the absent gods. Because he didn't think he could bear to hit her again for it.

She discovered a sudden fascination for the woodgrain on the tabletop, and spoke to it as if whispering secrets to a friend. "Edger did knock over the lamp in the loft, like I said, jumping around on the hay like you'd told him not to do 'cause it spoils the hay. And I was down grooming Moon in his stall, just like I said. But... Mama, when she'd turned him out of the house to go make noise elsewhere, 'd told me to *watch him.*" A long inhalation through her nose. "And I didn't, for those few minutes, and then it was too late." Her head came back up. "But I *for sure* didn't knock over the lamp myself, like *he* said, and everyone believed just 'cause he was coughing and crying and dyin', and I wasn't."

Fid pressed his palms to his face and scrubbed. Barr didn't think it helped any. "Nobody," he sighed at last, "could ever control Edjer when he got in that wild mood. He'd go till he dropped, and we picked him up and stuffed him in his bed anyhow, unwashed. I just hoped he'd outgrow it, in time, before he got too big to hoist. Although if there was a one of you I figured for most likely to run away to the river someday, he was it." He cradled his chin in his linked hands, looking depressed.

Forgiveness of a sort, Barr supposed, as good as anyone was going to gain out of the webbed tangle. At least the hard knot in Lily's ground eased a trifle, like an overtight muscle giving up under the pressure of a thumb; aching better. She didn't ask for more.

Barr rolled his shoulders and stretched his arms up, trying not to groan. He felt as beaten as if he'd dismounted from a long day of patrolling. In the rain. *I needed to have done this better.* It was a lot to ask of twenty minutes of truth, to lance an infection years in the brewing. *I want to do better.*

I have to do better.

"So. That brings us back around to Lily. Given her Lakewalker powers coming on as strong as they are, she needs training. She needs to be around other Lakewalkers, to show her how to go on. She needs to stay here. She can't go back to your farm." Leaving aside that she'd fight like a wildcat to resist such a returning, right now.

That was...maybe a little too blunt, judging from how Fid ruffled up. But any mealy-mouthed hedging Barr could imagine coming up with had to boil down to the same facts in the end. There wasn't much honesty in pretending Lily had a choice in this, except a little in *where:* Pearl Riffle, Clearcreek, some other camp. And Barr couldn't patrol out of Clearcreek, and in any other camp he would have even less clout, without the kin support they both needed.

And that's only the beginning of how hard our trail can be to ride. Lily needed to know this. Fid, maybe, could make do with the softer version, until Lily was ready to tell him someday herself.

Fid, too, stared down at the table, finding some echoing fascination in what he wasn't seeing in the grain. Barr could just about sense him laboriously reworking his every expectation for the results of his anxious journey, and his respect for the man rose a notch. Another notch.

"Lily," he said at last, "isn't really a child anymore, hard as it is for me to see it with my head full of memories. Girls only a little older than her get betrothed, some of them. Bell was only three years older than Lily is now when she *had* Lily; married and running her own household, too." Fid contemplated that statement with his own sort of paternal bewilderment. "And I truly don't know what it's like to be Lakewalker, on the inside." He looked up. "It was a long way to travel to realize it, but I believe I have to let Lily choose." Barr wondered if Fid was also thinking, *I needed to have done this better.*

"Do I really have a say?" asked Lily. Her rhetorical tone suggested she understood the catch. Already. *Good.* Which was not the same thing as happy.

"Only whether to do it half-hearted or whole," said Barr.

"Or throw myself in the river, I suppose." Barr wasn't sure if that was a snarl or a scoff. "Which I gather would be considered a sinful *waste.*"

Wait, had she actually just made a patroller joke? He offered in return, "That it surely would."

"Well, I'm not having any waste in my house. Tent. Whichever."

And cranky, it seemed, was not the same thing as *un*happy.

"Glad to hear it," murmured Amma from the side, and Lily's head swiveled around to meet her gray glare. They nodded to each other, as if in some mutual agreement. *What?*

So even Amma, it appeared, was not wholly immune to youthful admiration. Scary...

Barr didn't think there was any more he could do at this table today, and they'd drunk all the tea. A decent escape suggested itself. He tossed out, "I, uh, notice that deep burn on your right hand is giving you trouble still. If you like, I could walk you over to our medicine tent, and have one of our makers take a look at it before you go."

Fid looked surprised, touching his right arm gingerly with his left. "Like what you did for me before you left Hackberry? I have to admit, I do think that helped some."

It might be the reason he hadn't already lost a hand or arm to infection, although Barr would make no claims. "Verel or Yina can do a whole lot more than I could. I'm just a clumsy patroller when it comes to groundwork. They can fix up hurts way worse'n this one." He tapped his neck, and Fid squinted in curiosity. Barr rose, by way of leading, and Fid and Lily followed on tamely.

Amma observed from behind her desk, "There's a passable rivermen's inn down at Pearl Bend, Mister Mason, where you and your boy might find a room to rest up tonight before you start home."

"Uh, thank you, that's good to know."

Barr thought Fid took her prompting with fair tolerance, which cleared the last of Barr's mess from Amma's desk from her vantage. He breathed relief that he wasn't expected to find the farmers a place to sleep in crowded Tent Foxbrush.

He ushered his charges out, pausing at Amma's lifted hand to stick his head back in the door.

She stared at him for a thoughtful, unsmiling moment, but then said, "You did all right, Barr."

It wasn't delivered in quite the cordial tone as she'd praised him for the malice sighting, but he wasn't going to hold out for a miracle. He gave her a short nod in thanks, and retreated while he still had his skin. And, more importantly, his place in the patrol, and all the support that came with it.

Farmers, Barr had found, often didn't quite realize that patrolling wasn't a job of work like a field hand or a boatman. His labor was itself a donation from his tent, just like all his clothing and gear. His hand touched his belt. *And our knives, bonded or primed, donations of our bodies and lives.* Not something that could be counted in coin.

Not something that dared be counted at all, until the long debt of the malice infection was paid down even, one death shared with every monster at the last. Barr, like most Lakewalkers, had wondered if that barely understood legacy of their lost mage ancestors would be eradicated in his lifetime, and, like most Lakewalkers, had learned not to think too hard about it. The futile anticipation just made a fellow cranky.

FID WAS RIGHT fascinated by the medicine tent, and Verel responded with a genial lecture about medicine making while he worked over Fid's hand, and how the services were being cautiously extended to the farmer neighbors. Fid seemed to take in maybe one word in three of the first, but followed the second with a thinking look on his face. The scorings the mud-man had put on Barr's neck led naturally to the story of the malice sighting, which Barr let Lily mainly tell, and then back to how he'd found her in the woods, lightly touched on. Lily was already beginning to grasp what details were best left out to a non-patroller listener, Barr was reassured to find.

Barr managed to limit Fid's natural curiosity about where his all-but-daughter would be staying to a view of Tent Foxbrush from a distance. He did offer the tidbit, also welcome tidings to Lily, that Barr's mother was figuring out how to set her up a bunk alongside Raki's when his middle sister Toshi took over the old girls' room. No more temporary bedroll on the floor. Barr considered it a sneaky victory that he'd never had to beg outright, though he and Bay had been detailed to do the bed-building.

After a cast around, they found Reeve down watching the ferry with that river-hungry look on his face so common to youngsters seeing the Grace for the first time, which at least gave Fid something fresh to worry about. Barr raised his standing in the boy's eyes with a severely curtailed account of his own trip all the way to the Graymouth, most of which was new to Lily as well. This occupied the time till he was able to collect their horses and gear and ease them back to the south camp gate.

"Are there any messages you want me to give your mother?" Fid asked Lily.

Her lips flattened; she shook her head, but then managed, "Just tell her I'm going to be fine here."

Which was what Bell's heart most needed to hear, Barr supposed, that Lily was sheltered and well. *At her side* was a picture disastrous for both. Not so much peace, then, as a truce best preserved at a distance. For now.

"This isn't a goodbye forever," Barr pointed out. "You folks may travel this way again sometime. People could write.

And if Lily ever goes for a patroller, well, Hackberry Corner is in one of our patrol sectors." Which was how this had all got started in the first place, speaking of thorny reminders. "She might be able to stop in for a visit, between duties."

By her expression, Lily was not yet ready to regard this offer as a treat, but time changed all things. Given enough of it.

"And you, Patroller?" Fid's eyebrows lifted, a bit dryly. "Anything more you want said?"

Blight, no. If he couldn't heal Bell's wounds, the least he could do was not pick at her scabs. "Just tell her I'll look out for Lily. With everything in my abilities."

A quick fierce chin-duck. "See you do."

The hug at his stirrup Fid exchanged with Lily was awkward on both sides. Lily muttered a shaky, suffocated *Thank you.* Fid patted her clumsily on the shoulder in lieu of any more stab at words. It felt like blessing enough.

The two Masons mounted and rode toward Pearl Bend, with everyone waving a dutiful last hand, even Reeve, who was looking somewhat confused by the day's developments. Barr was entirely willing to leave Fid to cut and sew whatever explanations he chose for all this to Reeve.

He sneaked a glance at Lily's sober profile, watching them ride off. "You going to be all right?"

She shrugged. "In time. I expect."

"Can't ask for more. Let's go home."

They turned back to the camp, walking together slow.

EPILOGUE

THE Pearl Riffle bone shack, lair of the camp's knife-maker, lay as hidden as it could be in the heart of the camp. Which wasn't all that concealed, since the patch of woods in the shallow ravine that cut down from the valley's ridge was pretty small. The paths winding back and forth up into it tried to suggest a graver journey than the number of steps actually accounted for, to put the supplicant in the right frame of mind, maybe.

Lily, walking ahead of Barr, had an eager spring in her stride that he remembered from his own trek up this track, gods, it really *was* twenty years back, wasn't it? At the time, he'd seen getting his bonded knife as his portal into adult-hood, outward and visible sign of a maturity that he hadn't, actually, quite achieved yet. But you had to start somewhere. For Lily, it bore the added weight of marking full acceptance into her adopted community, absolute proof of her right to be there.

He'd been sixteen then; she was sixteen now. Why did she seem so unfairly *young*? She'd grown physically, to be sure, in the last two years since he'd brought her home to Tent Foxbrush. At first it had mainly gone into a gangling and somewhat alarming height, but then she'd filled out into her woman's shape. Watching her full hips sway as her strong legs boosted her up the hillside, her blond braid swinging in counterpoint, made Barr want to leap between her and every young male just like himself who'd ever been whelped. If only she hadn't made it so clear she was entirely capable of defending herself. With extra tutorials from her amused mentor Amma, absent gods help the coming herd of moonstruck fellows due to be slaughtered in her path.

He remembered his own father escorting him up this trail, trudging with slow steps that Barr had been sure were put on just to aggravate him. Now he and Oris Foxbrush trudged in tandem. He glanced over his shoulder. The graying patrol leader had a weird little smile on his face, watching Barr in turn.

"What," muttered Barr.

"Just thinkin'. You?"

"...Yeah."

The bare black branches of the late-winter trees seemed to clutch at the turning world like the fingers of a jealous lover, unwilling to relinquish what was already gone. They'd change to shy budding in the first warm week, but right now they suited Barr's mood a little too well. The path took one last turn through the boles to reveal the tiny clearing and the bone shack in its midst.

A one-room log cabin, any farmer would call it; barely more than shed-sized, though it sported costly glass windows for the light. The traditional south-facing leather flap was raised on its poles, letting more light into the bonecrafter's intensely private workspace. Smoke trickled up from the fieldstone chimney, whether for some of the rites of preparation or just to take the chill off the maker's fingers Barr couldn't guess. Feris Nighthawk, the maker, would have fasted and meditated this morning in preparation for this.

Along the eaves, a dozen thighbones and a few robust upper arm bones cured in the cold air, like sinister wind chimes. Each bore a carefully inked label somewhere on its length naming the donor, and the inheritor if there was one. Together with any final brief remarks it had tickled the donor to make, ranging from earnest hopes to last words in some fool argument to really bad jokes. A few people willed their bones to the camp generally, to serve whoever needed a bonded knife. Barr knew a fellow patroller with one; the words burned into the finished blade read simply, USE ME. The death it was meant to ensnare hadn't yet come up, though he'd carried it for years.

The thighbone for Lily's knife had been brought down from Log Hollow by Yina on her last visit home, Yina's share from a Tent Mink great-uncle and a generous gift. Farmer brides, Barr dimly thought, received bedlinens and cookware and such for their wedding portions, or a few farm animals, or seed grain. Baby blankets, maybe, if things had got far enough. Gifts for life. *We get dry bones, and are grateful for them.*

All right, Yina had brought back a cartload of other useful items for a new tent as well, which Barr knew because he'd unloaded them all. *Be fair.*

The bone blank had been delivered to Feris a month ago, the delicate groundwork for someday capturing a death to be laid in along with the carving and shaping, polishing and grinding to a heart-piercing point. Word had come down the hill yesterday that it was ready, and so here they all were. Ready or not.

Feris came to the entryway, smiling at Lily. "Good morning, Miss Mason. Are you all set for this? Feeling well today?"

"Yes, sir!" She smiled back, rolling on her toes as if to take flight. Barr was secretly pleased Lily had chosen to keep her farmer surname, though he gathered it was half for just how confusing she'd found Lakewalker tent-name-swapping customs. He pictured a future Tent Mason, rising up defiantly, and smirked.

Feris allowed Barr and Oris an ambiguous smile, waving toward the split-log bench across the clearing from his doorway. "Have a seat." The tent flap dropped closed emphatically behind him and Lily. Feris had mage-worked knife bone for Pearl Riffle for the past fifteen years, honing all aspects of his task to a courteous and necessary efficiency. When he finished this morning, he'd spend the rest of the day sagging in exhaustion.

Barr and Oris sat on the bench with matching grunts, which made Barr laugh under his breath.

"How are you holding up?" asked Oris.

"I'd think that's what we should be asking Lily."

Oris snorted. "It never is. Giddy-drunk on heroism, the lot of you, and never looking back. Just on."

"Not…very far on, seems to me now."

"Yeah. I remember how all-fired eager you were, rushing headlong half-ready."

"I was too all-ready!" Barr protested.

"Hah."

Barr dug in the damp, cold dirt with the toe of his boot. No insect or frog song yet broke the woods' chill silence, and bird chirps were still rare and lonely. "Does this get easier? With practice?"

"The waiting out here, you mean? I had the five of you, and a couple of your cousins—well, I misspoke, it was Kiska came up with Shirri, and your grandmother. Enough that if it was going to get easier, it should have by the time I was down to you."

"And…?"

"No," said Oris baldly. "Actually, as I recollect, you were the worst. Because it seemed to us you were the most likely of all to end up coming back early to haunt us as a primed knife. I knew I didn't want to be the one to carry it, if so. Thought maybe I'd give you to Amma to portion out."

"That would have been all right."

"Not from your mother's point of view." And, gruffly, "Or mine."

"Mm." Barr tilted his head, listening.

"Waiting for the yelp?" asked his father.

When the knife-maker sliced his thin scalpel across the recipient's arm to release and capture the live blood needed to bind spirit to bone blade, ground to groundwork. "With Lily, I imagine I wait in vain. I'll bet she doesn't even peep."

"*You* yelped."

"Did not. Must have been one of the others."

Oris snickered. "No, it was you. I remember, because I flinched and braced for trouble. Your next trouble."

"Well, for that you had to wait a while longer."

"A little longer."

"Not poking there," said Barr, attempting dignity.

"No, you wouldn't win."

The sun warmed the backs of their necks a little, burning wanly through the cloud veil.

"I hope," Barr sighed after a while, "it'll be a hundred years before Lily comes to prime her blade." After Barr was long buried, by preference. Though Lakewalkers didn't habitually carry their bonded knives about their persons for, quite precisely, a lifetime in *expectation* of dying in bed.

"So we all say," agreed Oris.

Barr turned the wedding braid on his left wrist, still stiff and new, threads bright-colored. String-bound to Yina through it, he could feel the life in her as she moved about her tasks somewhere in the camp below. Busy, engaged; he did love her intense focus, the wicked wit he'd discovered behind her straight face, her deep, deep ground. He wondered what oddness she was feeling of him right this moment.

They had hopes of a child; certainly they were having fun trying for one. Children, in time. Would he, for every celebrated birth, be constrained sixteen years later to sit again on a bench like this outside a bone shack?

"This is wrong," he said suddenly.

"Hm?" said Oris.

"Feeding our children into this long war. It should be us, not them."

"You are them." Oris huffed, the nippy air making his irony visible as a wisp of mist. "I suppose I was too, once, from somebody's point of view. Everybody born, dies. If you choose the first, you have already chosen the second."

Barr was pretty sure he hadn't felt the full force of what that meant till now, and he'd participated in every other part of this ritual, up to and including helping a dying friend to share. He stared at the blank leather of the tent flap, not needing groundsense to know exactly what was happening inside. Experience served. "Almost makes me wish I could have left her on her farm."

Oris grimaced. "Farmers die too. Die too young, too stupid, too messy, too old, too sick, same as us. No help for you there. Ours just get to be one knife-stick less meaningless, is all. A gift of sorts."

"...I didn't know I'd hate it this much."

"I thought you might."

Barr's brows rose, considering that. He tilted his head back and stared at the grim gray sky. "Lily likes having a grandfather, I hope you know. I gather they were in short supply in her family back at Hackberry Corner, so you got to be a novelty. Thanks for coming up here for her."

Oris shrugged one shoulder, as if half disputing this. "I didn't come up for her...well, not just for her. I figured this would make you fit to be tied. For the rowdiest blighted cub in our den, Kiska always said you had too wide of a sensitive streak. She was worried about you, today."

Barr's lips twitched. "Kiska was, huh?"

"Hush," growled Oris, though his eyelids crinkled just a bit.

They sat in unusually companionable silence until the tent flap lifted again.

"On your feet, Patrol Leader Mink," Oris murmured. "Time to be proud."

In the face of Lily's thrill as she held up her new knife, her new status, for his approval and praise, Barr had no trouble producing a smile. It was as simple as being a mirror reflecting the light. "That I am."